DOWN AT THE RIVER

THOMAS TIMMINS

DOWN AT THE RIVER

Book three of

THE HOUR
BETWEEN
ONE AND TWO

A mystery in three books

THOMAS TIMMINS

Zoëtown Media
Haydenville, Massachusetts

ZOËTOWN MEDIA

Down at the River
Copyright © 2014 by Thomas Timmins

Cover: Tom Dudley

Zoëtown Media ISBN: 978-0-9893283-2-6

Printed in the United States of America

Disclaimer

The author admits to taking a decade-long trip through the humid world of tofu making and marketing. He met countless inspired, industrious, good and eccentric people as he and his cohorts transformed soybeans into food for human beings. While some may wish to attribute familiar identities to some of the characters, living or dead, this is not a memoir. It is a work of fiction, arising from the author's imagination. Like all tall tales, it has at best a metaphoric relationship with what we perceive as the everyday world. If you find truth and pleasure in this book, they are yours to enjoy. That would make the author happy as the tofu master who, after stirring endless circles in a cauldron of hot soymilk, whips up a tasty batch of tofu he can serve to the world.

ACKNOWLEDGEMENTS:

Joe Timmins, David Grant, Angela Borda, Nancy Shobe, Barbara Sachs, Judith Rubenstein, Amy Swisher, Thomas Dudley all had sensitive and caring hands in the making of this book. Without Judith Roberts, Richard and Kathy Leviton, Madeleine Fox, Jon Lee, Vinny Natale, Maggie Stebbins, Cory Greenberg, Donnie Nelson, Mary Houghton and hundreds of crew members and thousands of imaginative and intrepid tofu aficionados, the author could never have made the astonishing journey from soybean slinger to tofu tale teller. I thank each one of you.

Contents

Chapter One

Charlie

BLACKMAIL

*we knew it was coming
but what could we do? he
thinks he's got me, ha!*

A few minutes after I got back from lunch, Benko walked into my office without knocking. I spotted his shoe so I knew it was him before he came all the way in. He shut the door, and locked it behind him and I kept my head down, watching his reflection in the stainless steel base of my desk lamp. He stood leaning against the door until I finally said, "Yeah?"

"Production's going good, boss."

"Yeah, Benko, I know. That's your job. What do you want?"

"About that book? You got a good offer?"

I flashed a cold look at him, in his stained production whites, wearing short sleeves to show off his muscles, with a floppy net holding his hair off his forehead. I said, "Get that shit-eating grin off your face. I don't have a number for you because you don't have anything for me."

"You don't believe that. You know what I have and you need it. I give it to you. Cheap. Five hundred."

"Five hundred?" I said, half in shock. I thought he'd ask for ten thousand at least. "Go home right now. Get that book and bring it back and I'll have five crisp hundred dollar bills waiting, right here on the desk."

He laughed and laughed. Then he sat down on my couch and leaned back and crossed his legs. He spread his arms across the span of the couch and clenched his cucumber-sized fingers. A pulse rippled up his arms from his wrist to his biceps and disappeared under the sleeves.

"Thousand, boss. Five hundred thousand."

Flabbergasted, I sat still and closed my eyes.

"Cat got the tongue?" Gladonov said. "Five hundred by February."

He's playing a power card, but hang in, be hard.

"You're an idiot, Gladonov. You want to blackmail me, go ahead. I was thinking ten thousand was a high number."

He laughed again. "This is big company, boss. Make lot of tofu, lot of money. I see my workers' payroll every week. Figure office pay is pretty big. You, Nora, Genevieve, me, we make good pay. Right now, it's a record sales. You skim a little, hand it over to Russian friend. Save your ass."

"I'm not rich, Benko. Everything that comes in goes out the next day to pay bills. Anything extra goes to paying our people good wages, benefits, schooling."

"Bullshit. Your house, this factory. Record sales."

"Not bullshit. If you knew anything about business, you'd know we have assets, all mortgaged, and we don't have cash. I couldn't even get you fifty thousand from profits."

Benko leaned forward with his paws gripping his thighs and stared at the floor. As he pushed himself to his feet, he said, "Sounds like we're close," then he walked away. As he unlocked and opened the door, he said, "Four hundred, done deal. Like they say."

"Fuck you, Benko," I said.

"We talk later, Charlie."

He left my office and just before he closed the door, he shoved it open again.

"I like you, Charlie. Very nice wife. Nice kids, too. You don't want jail. It's bad place for soft guy. Tell you what? Make business deal: I run production for Chinese New Year, you make big money. Give me two-fifty at end of sale, another one, one-fifty in a month, I go. You stay out of jail. Deal?"

We were getting somewhere, and I figured he'd take two hundred, maybe one-seventy-five by the time we finished dealing. I might be able to handle one fifty if I hocked everything and tossed in some of Meng's boon, but at that moment, he disgusted me and I lost my temper. I snarled at him. "Fuck you. You're fired."

He grinned and came back into the office. "Be careful, Charlie. Nobody makes production hum like me."

"I'll appoint Jorge or, hell, Nancy can do everything you do. I'm not stupid, Gladonov. I have back-ups in place."

He knew I was bluffing.

"Sure. Tell me about it. Who knows electricity? Who keeps steam boiler up when electricity goes down?"

Only one guy in the whole company could keep the electricity running. The same guy who could shut it down and keep it off. If he didn't get what he wanted in cash, he'd take it some other way.

I stared at him until he said, "One last thing. You don't want the diary, you know who does. I don't mean Nora."

He closed the door quietly, whistling as he went down the long hall toward production.

***

I called Nora and told her to take the kids to her mom's. I'd be home in twenty minutes. We had to talk.

As soon as I came in the door, Nora said, "What happened, Charlie?"

"Benko," I growled, taking off my coat. I was fuming.

"Benko? What did he do? What did he tell you?"

"He didn't do anything, yet. It's what he plans to do. He wants five hundred thousand dollars or he gives the diary to the Chief. He might sabotage the plant, too."

"Five hundred thousand? Where does he think we'll get that?" Nora's voice trembled.

"I'll tell you when I get home. Take the kids to your mom's. I'm almost finished here and I'm out the door."

***

An ugly sky squatted on the tops of the house and the bare sycamore and oak bordering our property. At least the low-pressure system raised the temperature above freezing for the first time in a month. All of upstate New York could get a foot of wet snow during the night.

Nora was in the kitchen brewing coffee when I came in. Without speaking, I hung up my coat and hat and walked over to her. When I hugged her, trying to establish our togetherness against Benko, she didn't stop shivering. It was infectious and shudders ran through me, too. I turned the thermostat up to eighty.

We carried our cups into the living room where Nora had built a fire in the fireplace. I spiked my coffee with a shot of Maker's Mark and stared into the flames. Nora sat on the edge of her chair, tapping her heel on the maple floor. I inhaled the sweet peppery fragrance of the burning birch and turned around. She was still shaking.

Nora stood up and crossed the room to the liquor cabinet. "I better join you for this one." She poured herself a splash of the bourbon in a glass. "Sit down, Charlie. You're making me way too nervous standing there."

"I don't know if I can." I sat down and got right back up. "I can't talk sitting down."

Nora shrugged and raised her glass to me. "Whatever. Walk. Talk. Tell me what's going on."

"He sent an email asking for a meeting. I knew what it was about. Let him come, I thought. I told him to see me in my office after lunch—my turf, my time."

I told her the whole story, ending with his threat to disable the factory if I didn't give him the ransom.

"He has me by both balls, now. The plant and the Chief."

Nora ignored my comment and said, "Is it true? Is he the only one who can handle the electricity?"

I snapped back. "Yes, goddam it. It's complex. We're too small to afford two skilled electricians on staff."

"I wasn't accusing you."

"Benko meant if I fired him, he'd sabotage the plant, cut the electricity."

"He wouldn't."

"What world do you live in?" For all her numbers and business acumen, Nora could be so naive about people.

"I'll talk to him," she said, pouring herself another finger of whiskey. Tossing a log onto the fire and settling herself on a footstool in front of the fireplace, she stared into the orange blaze. "He'll listen to reason. He and I have always had good communications."

"Stay away from him. I don't trust him. If he comes near you, call me. I'll handle Gladonov."

I hadn't told her about the cash Meng sent me, and before I dipped into it to ransom the diary, I'd try waiting Gladonov out. I'd had twenty years of negotiating experience and, unless he resorted to violence, I was sure I could beat him down to a reasonable fee. I might have to pay, but I'd pay as little as I could.

As I started toward the liquor cabinet, Nora rose and put her arm around my waist and lay her head on my shoulder. Her breath smelled sweet with bourbon.

"We'll figure it out, Charlie."

"It's a business battle, Nora. We win this one, we're home free." I lifted my arm over her head and dropped it around her, pulling her gently to me.

After a minute, she said, "Hey, look out the window. It's started."

In the west, the sky had turned blue but over our house the clouds had opened. Fat snowflakes sputtered down with deceptive delicacy.

I said, "I bet we'll get a foot by dawn."

With her ear still pressed against my chest, over my heart, she said, "Let's go for a walk before it gets dark."

"What about the kids?" I said, not wanting to leave them stranded during a blizzard, even with grandma.

"We'll walk first, then we'll pick them up, come home and roast marshmallows."

"God, Nora. I don't know how you can be so playful at a time like this."

"Don't worry, Charlie. I'm not feeling playful. This is survival. Hunker down with family on a snowy night. That's common sense."

***

I checked the thermometer outside the kitchen window. The temperature had dropped to twenty-three, perfect for an all night snowstorm. I retrieved Nora's and my down jackets and brought them to where she waited.

"You know, honey. It's strange," I said. "I feel good, well, not exactly good, but mentally clear. Benko started the bidding, laid out his hand, and said, come on, Charlie, your bet. Now I know about what he wants and his position, we have a good chance of working this out."

Nora sat down on the stool she kept by the serving island in the kitchen.

"Hey, let's go," I said, tossing her a coat. "Before it gets too slippery out."

She caught the coat and lay it on the island. "Take your coat off, Charlie. Sit down."

"What? I thought you wanted to go walking? We can figure out a plan to get the diary."

"Not yet. You said you knew a lot more about him? And that improved our odds?"

"Of course." Nora had become her serious and distant self again. "Don't tell me you know something else, something I don't." I sat down and bounced back up, searching for my glass.

When I couldn't find it, I went over to the island and sat on the stool across from her. "So?"

Nora raised her eyes to the ceiling, then, with her chin in her hand, she glanced around the room.

"You're making me nervous now, Nora. What?"

"All right," she said, her brown eyes liquid and sad. "You have to know this."

My heart started thumping in my ears. I was afraid of what she would say.

"I'm really sorry, Charlie. You know how I didn't come down on you when you told me you slept with Becky? I kind of accepted it and said let's make the best of it?"

"Yeah. By then, what else could we do? Benko had the diary." "And I'm one hundred per cent supporting you in the investigation?"

Uhoh, here it comes. Fee fi fo fum, don't get yourself bummed.

"Why are you saying this?"

"Remember, I never tried to hurt you. I made a mistake but it wasn't because I had bad feelings about you."

"What mistake?"

"I slept with Benko."

"You slept with Benko?"

"I'm sorry. Yes."

Could it be any worse? Only riding in the back of a hearse.

My throat clutched and I gagged. Sputtering, I groaned, "How could you? How could you? Gladonov?" She tried to take my hand but I jerked it away and slammed my palm into the refrigerator door.

Nora called after me, as if I were already out of the house. "I couldn't help it, Charlie. You weren't interested in me. He paid attention to me. I wanted a summertime fling, that's all. You had one. Yours ended in total disaster."

How could I deny that? I didn't try. Instead, I shouted, "The lowest snake in the grass is fucking my wife. How the fuck could you do that with that criminal?"

Nora stayed quiet, sitting at the counter. She'd laid the coat on her lap and was playing with the fur collar while I ranted and raved.

I felt about an inch high but I wouldn't let her see that. "Where did you fuck him? Here? Right here on that fabulous oak island I had hand-made for you for five thousand dollars?"

Nora stood up. "Stop it, Charlie."

"Sure, I know where you fucked him. Right in front of our romantic fireplace?"

"Stop acting like a two year old. I'm sorry. It was a big mistake. It's over. It's been over."

I swung my arms and picked up my coat and threw it as hard as I could at the cupboards. Then I faced her and growled, "I bet you did it on our bed."

"No, never here," Nora said. "We only did it a few times. Like you and Becky."

The words I'd used to minimize my affair with Becky flew out of Nora's mouth and slapped me across my jaw.

I recoiled. "Oh. Like me and Becky ... like me and her."

No surprise. It's the old new age. You got it: open marriage.

I laughed, not a funny laugh, but a hard, sad laugh. "Nora, you and me," I said. "A couple of losers. We should never have got married. No wonder you wanted that open marriage crap."

"You're right. I know. But we are married and we both screwed up big time. I'm sorry. You're sorry. What else can we do?"

"All the time we're in therapy you're dicking Gladonov. Such a liar." She had me completely fooled. What's worse, Gladonov knew I didn't know about him and Nora. No wonder he smirked at me when he asked for half a million dollars. He'd already conned me out of something far more valuable.

Nora came across the kitchen to within a few feet of me, ready to don boxing gloves, if I wanted to, though she knew I'd never strike her.

She said, "Don't start that hypocrisy thing, Mr. Hypocrite. I was stupid, I admit it. But you were in therapy with me when you were fucking your employee. What's so honest about that?"

Our anger escalated and we started shouting until Nora walked out to the back yard and stood in the twilight, hugging herself. I watched her while I cooled off.

She said it was over with Benko. She wasn't leaving me for him. We were still a team. I wanted to keep it that way, at least until we got the diary. We'd get Benko gone and then we could sort out our lives.

I picked up her coat and slid down the back steps to bring it to her. I brushed the snow off her hair and sweater and settled the coat on her shoulders. I snugged it closed around her and said, "Look at us. What a strange pair."

For the first time, she started crying. I pulled her against me and said, "We can get through this somehow, Nora. We've made it this far. But it's gonna cost us."

"I know," she said. "We have to pay Benko now, don't we?"
"Pronto," I said. "The only question is, how much more?"

Chapter Two

Genevieve

"DRAGON STEW"

The Year of the Rooster started at dawn every morning that January. I didn't stop moving or talking all month as I clucked Charlie's Soy to the World message like a chicken gone berserk. Half the time, I wondered if I still had my head on my shoulders.

My sense of humor saved me. I told my men produce buyers they could call the promotion the Year of the Chick if they thought of me and made out big tofu orders.

I created a dozen new recipes for the Year of the Rooster, traveled the whole Northeast from Philadelphia to Portland, with side trips to Chicago, Denver, Miami, and Atlanta, appeared endlessly on TV and radio, talked non-stop with customers, all because Charlie had dedicated American Tofu to a life or death mission.

I had to create widespread positive feelings about the company that no matter what happened regarding Becky's death, the company would live on as the only brand in our customers' minds.

Every night until my trip began, I stayed close to Liam, helping him with his math project or reading with him or cheering at one of his swim tmeets. When he and his friends raced back and forth across the pool, I forgot all my worries. Screaming with all the parents perched on the bleachers beside the pool, I felt like a normal mom, enjoying the chill of a damp but proud swim team parent.

The morning I left town, I planted Liam with my friends Carla and Denise who promised they wouldn't let him out of their sight, and he'd never know it. I crossed my fingers that Benko would keep his distance, now that he was so occupied in the plant.

On January twenty-third, almost a week into a grueling trip, I fielded an emergency call from Nora just before I went on Providence public television's cooking show.

Nearly hyperventilating, she gasped. "Thank God I had your itinerary, Genevieve. Benko is gonna do it. What should I do now?" "Benko. What?"

"He'll take the diary to Buhrman unless we give him five hundred thousand dollars."

"Five hundred thousand dollars?"

"Charlie won't give him the money. He says we can't."

"Doesn't the company have it?"

"Not even close. Charlie says Benko doesn't deserve any-thing." Nora began crying. "I know we don't have all of it, but Charlie says he won't even negotiate. I told him to sell his new SUV for cash and he refuses."

"You have to tell Charlie about your affair with Benko," I said. "If he doesn't know that, he won't know how demonic Benko really is. He thinks he's got Benko under his control be-cause he writes his paycheck."

Nora didn't reply for a long minute while she thought it over one more time. She and I had rehearsed how she would tell Charlie, but she never committed to it. She was afraid Charlie would hate her because she'd betrayed him when he needed her most.

"I told him," she said.

"What happened?"

"He was furious. He stood there in the middle of the living room like I'd smacked him on the head with a hammer. His face went completely white and he started biting his mustache."

"Did he get physical?" I asked, fearing the worst.

"Charlie would never do that." A defensive note came into her voice. "He's not that kind. Besides, he feels so guilty about Becky, he almost said he understood about me and Benko. I know he hates me, though. As soon as he heard about our affair, he said we had no choice. We have to give Benko the money, as much as we can raise. It's the only way. We have to get Benko out of our lives."

"Stay calm, honey. It's between Charlie and Benko now. Nothing will happen while the factory's so busy. They'll try to psyche each other out, but I don't think Benko will make another move right away."

"I hope he waits," Nora said. You were right about my telling him. "He threatened to shut down the factory if Charlie didn't give him the money."

"Benko's not stupid. He won't bite the hand of the dog who feeds him."

Nora said, "That's what Charlie thinks, but you can't predict Benko."

"Maybe. They're calling me, Nora. Showtime in thirty seconds. I'll call you tonight." I hung up wondering what ruins I'd find when I returned to Clement.

***

I came back from the tour and shut out the world. I didn't unpack my clothes or organize the rolls of film I'd shot or sort out the videos of my TV shows. I collapsed.

The first night home with Liam, we celebrated with a dinner of hot fudge sundaes and big mugs of hot chocolate. He insisted on popping caramel corn for desert. Liam had sculpted a miniature set of red and blue pots and pans out of Femo to commemorate my new fame as a TV tofu cook and I gave him a little souvenir from each city I'd stayed in. He liked the miniature Liberty Bell best because it had a tongue that clanged the bell in high C.

"When I shake it fast, it sounds like the 'Next Level' magic gateway chimes in 'Ace Blastforce and Company.'"

As soon as I tucked Liam in and kissed him goodnight, he fell asleep, and I called Nora.

"Oh, sweetie. I'm so glad you're back. Charlie said you knocked 'em dead in every city on the East Coast."

"I brought back a lot of video and audio tapes. We can watch them together."

"Let's have a show for the employees. They can see what marketing does to keep them in jobs."

"That'll be fun."

"Gen, this Benko thing is driving us nuts. I haven't slept in a week."

"Nora, please, I'm wrecked. Let's not talk about business or Benko or anything bad. I can't take it. Right now, I feel like a bowl of beef consommé that's been left out overnight."

"Gross. Let's pretend everything's fine. I can't get the diary and the money off my mind and I've lost ten pounds since you left and if Charlie wasn't out somewhere I'd come right over."

"Ten pounds? You don't have ten pounds to lose."

"I've got the new foolproof diet. Call it the Benko Plan. You're so afraid you don't eat."

We laughed a little. "I've been on that one myself. But right now ... I'm gorging on family love. The only thing that really works in the long run."

"I wish I could," Nora said. "How is Liam? Did he survive without mom's cooking?"

"Didn't miss it. He's great," I said. "Made me a little Femo cooking kit for a welcome home."

"He really loves you. So grown up."

I replayed the media tour for her, regaling her with stories about the egotistic media chefs and TV personalities I'd met, the camera men at every station who offered me carte blanche with their lives, how my recipes were big hits everywhere, especially with the crews I fed after the shows.

"After Philly, I had my closing pitch down cold," I said. "I left them with a tofu cooking idea anyone can do."

"The stir fry thing?" Nora asked. "Throw it in a hot pan with veggies and plenty of garlic and stir?"

"Even that's too complicated. No, what I said was, 'Take your favorite recipe that uses a hearty sauce, spice up the sauce twice as much as usual, saute tofu in cubes and toss them into the sauce. Simmer and serve. Presto.'"

We talked and talked about anything except Benko and Charlie and the business. For that half hour, I felt ten years younger, as if Benko didn't exist, as if my whole life lay in front of me with a certainty of happiness for me and Liam.

***

Over the weekend I plotted the details of my exit from American Tofu. A few more weeks of watching the fruits of my Year of the Rooster toil pour in, one more recipe demo shin-dig for Wegmans, and I'd begin my permanent vacation from the world of soybeans, rapacious Russians, and small town police chiefs watching every move you make.

I stayed in bed twenty-fours hours, regaining my strength, then Nora and I met for lunch at her house to talk about Benko. I doubted we'd find anything funny now that I'd come back to reality. She presented me with a mug of fresh carrot-beet-ginger juice.

"I think I need something stronger."

We laughed. She opened a bottle of red wine and poured two large goblets. "Cheers."

"Cheers." We held hands and sipped our wine.

"Things are out of control with Benko," she said.

"I was afraid of it."

"Charlie's totally consumed by the blackmail." Then Nora suggested we move into the dining room where we sat at the round table and sipped wine.

She said, "Ever since I told Charlie about me and Benko, I feel like I'm barely in touch with the ground. My head feels like it's either behind or ahead of time. I'm here but only part of me."

"Sounds like jet lag," I said. "I feel that way after road trips."

"Charlie and I haven't talked about it since. We're sleeping in separate bedrooms now, but at least we're civil. He couldn't say anything to me about the affair and I didn't tell him any of the down and dirty."

"That was smart. If you did, he might have confronted him."

"I'll never tell Charlie the details," Nora said. "He'd lose his mind if he heard some of the things we did. He'd have Benko killed. He'd torture him first. We'd lose everything."

We both swallowed deep drinks of our wine. The cuckoo clock on the wall ticked as we leaned on our elbows. I chewed my lower lip. Nora wrung her hands.

"We negotiated the ransom to a hundred fifty thousand," she said, "down from his five hundred thousand. Then he raised it to a hundred-fifty plus all the company cash on hand, whatever's in the bank or at the office."

"Charlie told him we'd have to sell our house and get the bank involved because I had to use our property as security for the money we borrowed to buy the new tofu equipment. Our credit cards are maxed-out. He told Benko it would get really complicated and it might take twelve months. Benko believed him. Said he'd take a hundred-fifty as soon as Chinese New Year production was done."

"That's a lot," I nodded, glad that I wasn't an entrepreneur, always having everything I owned on the line.

"We have no choice," Nora said. "It's all set. Charlie plans to use the profits from the Chinese New Year sales. That's about half. He said he'd find the rest someplace else. We told Benko nothing could happen until March first, when the returns from the business would be in."

"That gives you a little time."

"He wants it by February tenth. Charlie thinks he'll sabotage the factory."

"The asshole. That's the end of next week. Do you have it?"
"Charlie says don't worry," she said. "I don't know."

"Have you seen the diary or a copy of it?" I asked.

"Charlie asked Benko to prove he had it, to show it to him. Trust me, you can, he says. What a laugh. But like Charlie says, what difference does it make? I had the affair with Benko. Charlie had the affair with Becky, so we might at well pay for our sins. We'll have the diary in our hands once we buy it. If there's no diary, better yet, Charlie says. He can beat Benko at any game he wants to play."

"Jesus. Pure testosterone talking."

"That's Charlie," Nora said. "He's not always the smartest when it comes to money."

I almost said, "Or women," catching myself before I belittled Nora. Instead, I asked, "If Benko's bluffing, why doesn't Charlie go to Buhrman, tell him everything? He can fire Benko and charge him with blackmail."

"Neither of us want our reputations ruined. Would you? The media was a flock of vultures when Becky died. What do you think they'd do if they found out about the diary or Benko and me?" Nora finished her wine with a big gulp.

"Yeah. I know. Biggest scandal outside Albany for years."

"They'd find out all right. The Chief would leak it and we'd lose the business. No customer would stay with us if they thought the owner was a womanizing murder suspect. Everyone would think Charlie killed her. We'd lose everything." She'd thought through all the sorry consequences. "What would you and Liam do?"

"I don't know." I wasn't ready to tell her that I'd be leaving Clement before long. I had to keep that secret until I landed a new job. I knew Benko hadn't revealed our affair to her because if he had, she'd have said something by now and Benko would have bragged to me that he told Charlie and Nora. He'd enjoy my shame about not letting my close friends know the whole foul truth about all of us.

"What if he takes the money and hands the diary over to the cops anyway?" I asked, moving the conversation ahead, wanting to slide by the possibility that Nora might know about Benko. If I were in her shoes, I'd expect her to tell me. On the other hand, I said to myself, I'd want to keep the situation as simple as possible. Besides, my affair with Benko had nothing to do with the blackmail.

Nora smiled at me, her eyebrows raised a fraction. "That's where we're hoping you'll help us."

"Help you? How?"

"We want you to make the exchange, the cash for diary."

A fist of fear thumped into my abdomen.

"Will you?" she asked, squeezing my fingers.

I stared at her, my stomach rumbling with wine souring the carrot juice. "I'm as scared of him as you are," I said. "When he kidnapped Liam at Niagra Falls, it showed he'll do anything."

"It was Benko's idea. He said you're the only one he trusts."

Benko had cornered me again. Maybe he had kept our affair secret, so far, but now I wondered. If Nora knew about us, would she tell me or would she play it the same way I did, keeping it secret?

Once I got involved, Benko would want something else from me besides Charlie and Nora's cash. Still, I had an irrational feeling I'd be safe because Benko would call me his only friend in Clement. If I was the money-bearer, he'd have to back off from me and Liam. So, always a foot soldier in the tofu wars, I agreed to carry the ransom and retrieve the diary.

Now that I entangled myself in whatever happened with the blackmail, I decided Charlie and Nora needed to know about my affair with Benko. If I didn't tell them soon, before the exchange, with the pressure they were under, they'd think the most paranoid thing possible: I was in collusion Benko.

When they heard, I expected Nora would feel hurt and Charlie mad, at first, then they'd understand how Benko had swooped through American Tofu like a raptor, piercing every little mouse and mole with his voracious beak, and dragging us away, bleeding and crying like the sorry prey we were.

Every winter, on the night before Chinese New Year, Charlie threw a party for the employees. That year he wanted something unforgettable, something to make everyone proud and steep them in American Tofu's mission.

A few nights after Nora asked me to carry the ransom to Benko, we sat in their living room, drinking tea and designing the menu, putting the final touches on the Year of the Rooster "Tofu To-Do" company bash. They'd asked me to make a photo documentary of the party for the company newsletter and web site.

"I will," I said. "But if the party's anything like last year's, I better shoot before they empty the punch bowl. We don't want everyone to look smashed out of their minds."

Charlie and Nora laughed. "Take a few later on, too," Charlie said. "For kicks. We won't publish them, but some of the crew might like to see themselves cutting loose."

I described the "Dragon Stew" I wanted to make for everyone.

"After tasting a bowl of the stew, the guys at every station claimed they could feel dragon energy in their ... You could see color rising in most of the women's faces, too."

Charlie just stared at me, a sour expression on his face. As he tossed back another slug of his drink, he muttered, "Sounds uplifting."

"We'll need to have our spirits uplifted after I tell you guys something you don't want to hear," I said. Without waiting for them to prepare themselves for bad news, I went on. "Benko and I had an affair last summer." I gazed at Nora with sorrow in my heart. "The same time you were doing it with him."

I felt sorry for Nora. Every person she loved had betrayed her: her best friend - me, her idiotic husband, her cruel lover. Worse, her own feelings for a scheming monster had nearly brought her and her family to ruin.

Nora opened her mouth and put her fingers between her teeth. Shivering, she sagged in her chair and bawled. Charlie's eyes blazed.

"This is fucked," he said. "Totally fucked. I should have known it. That settles it. We're all in this shit up to our throats."

"We can't blame ourselves," I said. "He's good. He fooled all of us. He played on our weaknesses and got what he wanted. We just have to be smarter than him from here on in."

Nora asked sadly, vaguely, "I wonder who he's sleeping with now?"

"It better not be you two!" Charlie shouted, standing up. "Tell me. You're not still fucking him are you?"

"Settle down, Charlie," I said, standing to face him. "You two are so emotional about this."

"God dammit, Genevieve. We're gonna get tarred and feathered. I end up in jail, my family's homeless in the middle of winter-you want us to be logical! Wake the fuck up!"

I barked right back. "Go work out your feelings with your therapist." Charlie could be so dense. "Benko is brilliant. Cold. We have to use our heads or we'll all lose everything. Not just money."

Charlie poured himself a drink of whiskey. Nora and I declined his offer.

"I have just as much to lose as you two. Think about it."

We sat staring at each other. Charlie gulped his drink.

"Yeah. All right," he said.

"Let's be rational," Nora said.

I doubted "rational" was possible for either of them. For me, either.

Charlie swilled the rest of his whiskey. "Right. Rational as chickens with a fox in the coop."

Nora's question about who he was sleeping with now gave me an idea. In the short time since I'd unloaded my secret, my mind had cleared. Benko was going to get away with the money. Was he getting away with murder, too? I hoped not. Becky's death had to be an accident, but at that moment, I couldn't put it past Benko.

"That's a good question, Nora," I said. "Who is he sleeping with now? It's got to be somebody. That pole he's got hanging between his legs runs his life. Have you talked to Bernice lately?"

"I'm too ashamed. I'm afraid she'll gossip about me." She sat on the couch, her knees tucked under, holding herself in her thin arms.

I never expected Nora to fall into self-pity. I pushed against her paralysis. "Forget it, Nora. You've got to risk the gossip. Call Bernice right now. She's our best bet to find out any rumors we can use against Benko. Get her to start telling you everything she knows about him. I'm going to listen in on the other phone."

"Me, too," Charlie said.

"You just sit with Nora while she's talking to Bernice." I had to order Charlie around, keep him in the background or he'd try to take charge and end up forgetting what's important. Playing macho man, confronting Benko, Charlie would lose. "I bet we hear some shocking things about our long-dong blackmailer. Your wife needs all the support you can give her. Maybe even some love, if you still can."

Chapter Three

Charlie

EVERYBODY KNOWS ALREADY

This is America, boys it
always comes back to
the pecker or the gun

The one guy I trusted, the jerk I depended on to keep my factory pumping out product, the sleazebag ends up as the guy who stabs me in the back.

I can't believe I missed it. Gladonov's practically running my business, I'm giving him bonuses, I'm laying on the booze and all the time, he's fucking my wife. Not only that, he was bonging the only woman I ever had a true love affair with, right while she's sleeping with me. If this guy'd had a chance, he'd have jumped Shu Ling. Maybe he did? My trusted second mate.

In my own house, when Genevieve revealed that Gladonov had been doing her, too, I lost faith in everyone.

Being one of the liveliest and most talented women I'd ever met, I'd always thought Genevieve was the most independent and powerful. I liked her as a saleswoman because she was used to getting whatever she wanted. She controlled her environment and the people in it and everybody loved her for it. When she'd told me about her affair with Giordano, I silently congratulated her for her guts.

A single mother living in a god-forsaken little town in the middle of nowhere, working her tail off, driving her car into the ground, Giordano could have meant total freedom for her. If Giordano wanted, he could support her in any way she desired, out of his petty cash, and never notice it. For her sake, I half-hoped she and Giordano would get permanently involved. For our sake, what better way to guarantee long-term tofu sales than to have your sales manager intimate with your best customer?

But when I heard she'd been involved with Gladonov, at the same time Nora was, I said to myself, why does everything come back to the pecker? He's a nothing, a flesh-and-blood wrench, a worker, a factory man, that's all. A big baboon nobody would ever miss if he was gone from the earth.

I'd never felt hate until I found out the truth about him and women. I wanted to kill him. Not only that, I had a duty to get rid of him. His death would solve all of my problems, the company's problems, save all the women in town from Gladonov's berserk prick.

I had three or four options, people who could help me make the contact. Giordano, Meng, a guy I knew from the Philadelphia produce market, or I'd take care of him myself.

Assign him some hazardous job at work, say, repairs to the 440 amp electrical service. Hit him "accidentally" with enough voltage to fry him to a cinder. We'd celebrate the Year of the Rooster by roasting that arrogant cock in his own juice. Or I'd get him under one of our trucks to fix the transmission and somehow knock it off the jack, squashing him like the roach he is.

As thoughts of revenge jetted around my brain, I realized I didn't know enough about the factory machines or trucks to entrap him. Besides, another dead worker in the shop could be the company's funeral. I decided on the straightforward, anonymous way: have him shot.

Under an alias with a New York City address, I would sub-scribe to a UPS box number in Albany and write to a classified in Global Mercenary that advertised "discrete jobs."

You're going too far, it's crazy, man. Do this, the Chief will have you rotting in the can.

I thought of going online until I realized how easy it would be to trace any emails back to me, if something went wrong. People were already watching me, I thought. Just because of the publicity around Becky's death.

Still, I didn't think anything short of putting Benko out of his misery would save any of us, until Genevieve persuaded Nora to call Bernice.

We all sat in my living room listening to Nora interview the woman like a professional reporter. Even though Nora said nothing about the blackmail, Bernice understood the stakes were high.

She told us everything she knew about Gladonov. He seemed distracted lately, she said. He'd bought a car and spent a lot of time out of town. Bernice claimed she didn't know who Benko was sleeping with now.

Genevieve passed Nora a note to ask the woman if she knew anything else about Becky and Benko.

"I told you about how she couldn't get him off her back?" Bernice replied. "All I know is she told me she was thinking about charging him with sex harassment."

"Bernice, did Becky ever say anything bad about Charlie?"

I almost peed my pants when she brought that up.

"No. She loved Charlie. She'd never had a better boss. Becky would have done anything for Charlie. We all would."

"Are you sure?"

Nora, I thought, stop pushing.

"Why do you think we put up with Gladonov? Charlie must have a good reason for keeping him. We can't figure out why he doesn't get rid of Benko. We don't need him. We can handle any production problems and fix the machines ourselves. Ben-ko treats us like dirt. We want a little decency."

"I'll tell Charlie," Nora said. "I'm sure he's working on it. He'll be glad to know how much you trust him."

Bernice cheered me when I heard her say "Charlie knows already, Nora, I'm sure he knows. We saw how broke up he was when Becky died. How good he treated her kids."

The conversation stopped while Nora read another note from Genevieve.

"Can I ask you one more question?"

"Sure. Anything to help."

"Did Becky ever show you her diary?"

"Diary? No. That's funny. Did she have a diary? She told me everything about herself, so I'm sure I would have known about it. She was a lot like me. We don't like to be alone and we like to talk. In a lot of ways, we were each other's diaries."

Nora thanked Bernice and said that she was so sorry that she'd lost her best friend. She asked her to keep their talk just between themselves.

"It's important for the company's future," she said.

"I get it, Nora. Don't worry. Nobody needs to know everybody's dirty laundry."

"You're such a good friend, Bernice. I'm sure Charlie will do everything he can to get a better plant manager, real soon. Ask everyone to be patient for a little longer."

She's no dumb broad. You oughta be proud.

The way she handled the interview, I'd be lucky to have her run AT's human resources full-time.

After the call, we all felt better, especially me. My people were still with me. I'd just found seventy allies I didn't know I had. The people were my production crew, not Gladonov's, and I'll let them know in spades tomorrow. I'd have plenty of character witnesses if Buhrman ever indicted me. I was sure Bernice's praise made Nora feel proud of me.

"You know," I said, "you were great, both of you. Great questions, great interview. I feel good."

"Don't get too secure, Charlie. Bernice knows you were sleeping with Becky," Genevieve said.

"What? She didn't say that. How do you know?"

"You better learn to listen between the lines. Becky told her everything? They were each other's diaries? Get it? She also said she wouldn't tell anyone and that means Buhrman. If she knows, I bet half the factory knows. We better hope they can all keep their mouths shut."

She held out her glass and I refilled it with *Gato 999*, one of my finest wines. We were drinking up my cellar, but what difference would it make if we didn't get Benko out of our lives.

"It doesn't mean Becky told her anything. She promised me she wouldn't." I glanced at Nora, sad to admit the depths of my deceit. Staring hard at Genevieve, she ignored me.

"Before you pay Benko off, get that diary," Genevieve said. "In fact, you better get him to show it to you before you agree to do anything. You better make sure it exists. If Bernice is right, the diary's just another Gladonov bluff. If it does, he must have made a bunch of copies."

We sat up past midnight talking and finished two bottles of eighty-dollar Cabernet. Our involvement in Becky's death and the paths we had to take to extricate ourselves had evolved into a complex maze of 'ifs' with no clear path out.

Genevieve's opinion was we didn't have proof that there was a diary. If as Bernice believed, Becky had plans to file a suit against Benko, that would be in the diary and he knew it. He'd be implicated in the death by her words.

Really good news was that if we got rid of Gladonov, whether we paid him off or he had an accident, no one in the plant would mind. In fact, they'd probably rally behind me and whatever I wanted to do. It wasn't a case of my honor—this was pure survival.

I tried to "listen between the lines" as Genevieve spoke. I thought I heard her imply that I, or someone, should go ahead and eliminate Gladonov. I was tempted to tell her about the steps I'd already decided on.

Nora suggested paying him off as soon as possible and telling him to stay out of our lives forever.

"We can pay him money," I said, "but if we don't have the diary, I'll never sleep at night".

Genevieve said, "We have to see that diary. If he doesn't have it or she didn't write anything about Charlie, we have a whole new future. Get him to show you a photocopy. At least a couple of pages."

"Yeah," Nora said. "If he really has it and we get it, we know who's in trouble, Charlie or Benko."

"Or both," Gen snapped.

I said, "I'm way ahead of you guys. I asked him for a copy to prove one really existed. He said he'd show one to me for a fifty thousand."

"Maybe it's worth it," Nora said.

"Maybe. Worst case? I give him fifty thousand dollars for blank sheets of paper. He wins big."

"But we'd know for sure."

"Not only that, we all know, he makes a bunch of copies. Then he blackmails us for the rest of our lives," I said.

"It's worth it," Nora said.

"You write him the check from your account, then. I won't." After listening to Bernice, I was sure Gladonov was bluffing and I wasn't about to pay him a cent for anything less than the real thing and proof we had all the copies, paper, on his hard drive, in the cloud. I'd have to have my genius IT guy make sure.

Gen got up out of her chair and knelt down between us, taking one of our hands in each of hers, lacing her fingers into ours and clenching.

"All right. Stop it. You're both right. Let's just get this over with. I'll be the transfer agent," she said. "It scares me to death. I give him the money, he gives me the diary. You be close by, Charlie, in case he tries anything funny. If he does, we'll give him the money and run as fast as we can."

Chapter Four

Genevieve

THE "TOFU-TO-DO" BASH

The night before our "Tofu-To-Do" party at Charlie's house, Jorge Riviera called me from San Francisco. He offered me the job of Vice President of Marketing and Research of his company *New Old World Foods*.

"Our friend Giordano told me I'd be crazy if I didn't hire you," he said. "So, if you want, the job's yours. I personally think this is one of the most exciting jobs in the whole food industry."

"It sounds great," I said.

"You'll have a chance to influence people's eating for years to come." His exuberance inspired me to imagine the new life he offered me. I saw myself zooming all over the world exploring every continent for exotic vegetables, fresh tastes, bringing back old ways of cooking and transforming them into modern menus. I'd photo-document them and publicize them on the internet the way I did the small farm women's lives and foods.

Liam would come with me on our mission to find original foods that humans have eaten for centuries and bring them back to the twenty-first century.

Barely on the ground, I said good night to Riviera and began to let my fantasies about San Francisco fly. I wandered to Liam's room and leaned against his open door, watching him sprawled in sleep, wishing I could wake him to tell him the news. Living in the Bay area had always been a dream of mine and I knew he'd learn to love our new life there.

When I tell my customers I get my inspiration from my son, I mean that I do what I do for his sake, but I also mean his energy and love of life excite me. He'd dive into San Francisco with the same zest he dives into the pool or makes friends wherever he goes.

I'd decided long ago that Liam would go to high school some place other than Clement. He deserved more than football, beer, and cruising the mile-long downtown strip for his adolescent education. With the salary Riviera offered, Liam would still be able to see his father as much as he wanted. My main worry was that when I traveled, I'd have to find somebody I could trust to stay with him.

Only two things stood in the way of a smooth transition to the new life. One: The Year of the Rooster, and that was just about done, as far as I was concerned.

And Benko. More than anything, we had to get Benko out of our lives.

***

Benko the swindler, acting the martyr, sought sympathy from everyone. He claimed he was so busy filling the record sales orders for the Chinese New Year he might not be able to come to the company party. He'd tried to have it postponed until after the New Year, so "the workers would be fresh" he claimed. But Charlie authorized as much overtime for all the workers as they needed to finish work well ahead of the party.

Charlie was sharp about his employees. With big checks and a party coming, the factory workers would be in great moods and they'd be on Charlie's side no matter how our scheming about Benko worked out.

I tried to stay away from Benko completely. When we accidentally saw each other in the factory or near the office copy machine, he always grinned and caressed my whole body with cold eyes. The first time he did it I turned my back.

"Nice bottom you have. Always my hands you can feel them good on it," he whispered.

"Shut up, Benko. Leave me alone."

If he came into the office to talk about some production issue, I kept my door wide open. We'd stopped talking on the phone once Nora told me about how he treated her, but I could feel his twisted mind calculating the best way to handle me as he carried out his plans for extracting the money from Charlie. I felt relieved he'd decided that putting pressure on me wouldn't help him with Charlie.

Once, approaching me in the warehouse and smiling, tossing his long hair like a whip, he said, "I'm available. Always for you, Genevieve. How about tonight?"

The way he snarled my name sent prickles of fear up my neck. After that, for the first time in my life, I locked my door every night.

***

Charlie called me into his office. I sat down on the couch and sighed.

He sighed with me, but held his body rigid in the chair.

"It's a bitch. The worst."

He looked to me for sympathy. I felt for him and Nora, but I couldn't afford to be emotional now. None of us could. We were past that. I nodded and reached over to hold his knee for a couple of seconds. Charlie relaxed a little.

"The Chief started another round of interviews with the staff," he said. "Some crazy idea he learned at a conference. He's asking everyone to submit to hypnosis. The hypnotist is going to take them back in time."

"That'll never hold up in court, Charlie."

"Doesn't matter. He'll scare the hell out of them. Everybody has secrets. He told Bernice everything he learned about the workers would be secret. Irrelevant. Unless of course someone admitted to a crime.”

"When's this supposed to happen?" I needed to know so I could get out of town before the Chief had someone put me under.

"Right after the New Year. Buhrman said the shrink who's gonna do the hypnosis said it's more effective when everyone's rested. Less resistance to the hypnosis. Christ. What next?"

"I'm surprised he hasn't called us all in for a lie detector test."

"It gets worse every minute," Charlie said, kicking the coffee table. His precious bowl of lucky soybeans tipped over, spilling the little tan globes across the carpet.

"So much for Soy to the World," I said, making a weak joke. Charlie gripped my hand and stared into my eyes.

After a long silence, he said, "It's not done, Gen. Never give up." I hugged him and eased out the door. Back in my office, I wept.

Charlie, Nora, and I devised a plan to find out if Benko really had the diary. If he did, Nora and I wanted to read it before Charlie gave him any money. In his high anxiety, we doubted he could tell the difference between a forgery and the real thing.

None of us could bear being with Benko alone. Even Charlie had taken to writing him memos and texts for all of their business communications. So our plan was to use the hubbub of the party crowd to protect Nora as she talked to him.

She'd tell him they had to read the diary before they could give him any money. Once they read it, he'd get half the money, as they agreed. The rest would come on March first. He could keep the diary until the final exchange of cash for the book. If he didn't let them read it first, he'd get nothing.

"What if he says 'no'?" Nora asked, her face tighter, revealing lines I'd never seen. She couldn't eat. She hardly drank water.

I said, "Then he's bluffing. Charlie should just fire him."

"Wait a minute," Charlie interjected. "He's way too tricky. I'm afraid even if we get the original diary, he'll blackmail us with a hidden copy whenever he needs cash. We're his freaking pension."

"He'll have to give me his hard drive. And any copies he has around," I said. "You can have your IT guy track down anything in the cloud and get rid of it."

Charlie looked doubtful. "He'll hide a copy somewhere."

"What other choice do we have?" Nora said.

She'd become so pessimistic and dispirited, I wondered if she could handle any conversation with Benko.

When Charlie muttered, "There's other ways ..." I said to myself, Shit. Don't let Charlie try something stupid. He doesn't understand he can't play the violence game with Benko.

"Let's just work our plan, like we do every day in business," I said. "If Benko says 'no,' we'll figure something out."

"Goddam it," Charlie said. "We can't cover all the bases. No matter what we do, it's risky. With enough money, we can handle Benko. I'm worried about the Chief if he ever hears anything from the crew about me and Becky. Jesus."

I picked up their hands again, held them like limp empty gloves. "We'll just have to do something and pray Benko takes the money and runs as far away as he can."

They both gripped my hands, both with weak, hopeless smiles on their faces. Even if our plan worked, we all knew Benko might come back for a second installment. At least by then, I'd be far away, living a new life. Even if I had to change my and Liam's names.

***

On party day, Nora had a migraine and she spent the afternoon in bed. She planned to greet people at the door, but then she would leave with the kids for her mother's where they'd spend the night. The closer party time came, the worse her head ached. Charlie drove her and the children to her mother's an hour before the first guests arrived.

I steeled myself to play Nora's role in the negotiation with Benko. Midway through the evening, when the noise level began to rise with the hard-driving dance music and high-pitched talk, I approached Benko, keeping my fear hidden behind an amiable face. He'd spent most of the evening sitting alone next to the piano, sipping from a half-concealed flask.

"Did you like the Dragon Stew?" I said.

The piece de resistance of my new recipes was a spicy tofu and seafood dish that was meant to fill you with euphoria. By the happy faces of everyone else in the room, I thought the recipe had worked.

"Didn't try it yet. My own 'Dragon Blood' I like very much," he said, pointing to the flask in his paw.

"By the way," he continued, "congratulations on selling so much tofu. Only you, in all the world, beautiful woman. You convince supermarket guys to buy so much." He smiled. "Of course, to get man to do whatever you want, you know how. I know." He grinned. He lowered his voice and leaned toward me. "Your victim any time. Just say."

Tempted to reply to his banter, I inhaled instead, and smiled warmly. "Benko, I know everything about you. I know you're a ten-faced hypocrite. You were never my victim. You're the one who has victims."

I felt half the people in the room watching us, turning their heads, glancing, turning away, and glancing over again. The buzz of talk diminished. Charlie stood behind the bar with his back turned, laughing loudly and clapping one of the men on the back. I turned my back to the party and whispered.

"Nora's sick, Benko. She asked me to talk with you." He nodded, still smiling, still playing along for the audience. "She said they'll give you the money you twant tomorrow but you have to show them the diary first and let them read it." He stopped smiling and glanced toward Charlie. "Then if everything's cool, you'll get the rest on schedule. If not, too bad."

He finished the half-glass of vodka he'd held buried in his paw. "Thank you so much, sales woman." He stood up, shoving his face close to mine, and mumbled so quietly only I could have heard him. "I have enjoyed our talk. Immensely like my heart enjoys you. Almost like I have enjoyed your mouth around the 'Amazing Russian Sausage.'"

I turned my head away from his septic breath, but he pinched my chin in his hand and turned it back, pulling me even closer.

Smiling as if he were telling a happy secret to a good friend, he groaned into my ear. "Same pleasure perhaps you can offer me again? Before I hand over diary. Why don't you check your book so we can arrange time. You can always find me in factory."

Fine drops of his spittle landed on my cheek. I expected vile comments, but he nauseated me to my toes.

"Excuse me," he said, still smiling, dropping my chin and turning around toward the bottle. "King Tofu I must speak with himself." His fist seized the vodka and he meandered through the crowd calling cheerfully, "Boss. Boss."

Charlie spotted him and tilted his head toward me, mimicking a question.

I raised my eyebrows and mouthed "I tried."

Benko and Charlie disappeared out the back door. While I waited, I stirred the remaining Dragon Stew. Bernice, a petite brunette wearing an iridescent blue body stocking and a white cashmere vest, worked her way toward me through the munchers at the counter.

"Benko is so hard to resist," she said as she ladled some stew into a bowl, "even if he is evil." She watched my face, holding my eyes in a long, knowledgeable stare. "I really like these scallops," she said casually, breaking the spell. "They taste so fresh."

I filled a small bowl and waited for her to go on. I had nothing to hide from Bernice. She was our secret ally.

"I can't talk with my mouth full," she said. "I wish I could cook like you, Genevieve."

"I'm coming out with a cookbook. I'll give you a copy," I said, keeping the double talk going.

"Oh. I always wanted to know how to make what I fix taste the way I bet you do." She moved closer to me, as if she wanted to speak in secret.

"It's easy." I went on. "You can make it taste like anything. That's how I sell it."

"People like your recipes. I never saw so many tofus fly out that factory as this year. Good overtime for all of us. We owe you."

"No. I'm just doing what I'm hired for."

"Ain't we all," Bernice said. She pulled me by the arm into the empty kitchen. "When are you going out of town again?"

"Soon. Why?"

"I'm just glad things are slowing down in the plant," Bernice said, running water from the sink spigot into her glass. "It's been awfully crazy in there lately. Some of the guys were worried about one of the grinders. They think Gladonov needs to put some time in on it. There's some real necessary work they've got to do. In a couple of days, then … you're out of town?"

"Always on the road," I said.

"Everything will be all right, Genevieve." She smiled, caressed my cheek with her callused little hand, and said, "Have a good trip. I'll see you when you get back."

Before I could say anything, she slipped away and disappeared into the living room, letting a burst of music pound into the kitchen before the door swung shut behind her, leaving me alone with the dulled thud of percussion.

What was that all about?

If she and the other workers were planning to take Benko into their own hands, I'd better warn her. I doubted any of the factory workers were clever enough to corner him. Not only that, if he saw them coming, he'd tincite someone to attack so he could hurt them, badly, claim self-defense, and somehow, find himself free and set up for life by lawyers and American Tofu's insurance company. Bernice and the crew deserved a warning. I pushed my way back into the party, searching for Bernice just as Charlie came in from outside, alone.

Jovial, carefree, he hugged half a dozen men and women as he made his way toward me. He reeled into my side, lodged a finger in my belt, whirled me around, and gave me a huge squeeze. Charlie and I were sometimes affectionate at work, so nobody paid any attention to us. I thought he'd drunk way too much for a company party with the liability he could have.

He held me as he whispered, "It's all set. We'll know in the morning." He kissed me vertically, half on the lips, half on my chin, and pirouetted away.

Momentarily relieved but doubtful, I snagged his collar and hauled him back. "What do you mean?"

"I'll tell you later. Don't worry. It's fine. I'm not drunk. I'm saving that for tomorrow night. Let me go. I gotta show everybody a good time. We meet Gladonov at his place at five thirty in the morning."

Charlie wove his way from person to person until he staggered onto the dance floor. I watched from the door for a while before one of the young warehousemen asked me to dance. We bounced around the room, bumping into everyone we passed, all in momentary release from our problems, whatever they were.

Bernice hurtled by me and I slipped away from my partner and angled myself in front of her. With her eyes half-closed, she was working hard against the blasting beat of some reggae star. I gripped her shoulders and put my mouth against her ear. "Don't try anything with Benko. He's dangerous."

She grinned and tickled my ribs with both her hands and whirled away. I watched her snuggle into a man's arms and grind her pelvis against him. I watched all the revelers, cutting loose in the boss's house. Ah, Chinese New Year's Eve. East meets West in rural New York and anything goes. For the rest of the party, American Tofu crammed itself into Charlie's living room to jerk and sweat and whoop out the old year and call in its own special New Year.

Charlie avoided me for the rest of the party, except to thank me when I came to say good-bye just before midnight. "Leaving so early?" He tried to slur but I could tell he was acting.

"You're picking me up before dawn and Liam has a swim meet tomorrow night. His mom needs sleep so she can cheer really loud after working a long day."

"Thanks for everything, Genevieve," Charlie said, walking me to the door. "I mean everything. The stew, taking Nora's place. The sales. The sales." He started to wax drunkenly rhapsodic. "If you hadn't sold so much, we'd never have had this party."

"We all did it, Charlie. Now," I said, gently circling my arm around his shoulder and pulling him close for a confidential chat, "what deal did you make with Benko?"

"The money for the diary. Like we said."

"You told him, first the book, then some money, right?"

"Well, I have to give him some of the money first but if he doesn't show me the diary, he won't get the rest." Charlie puckered his lips in a show of determination.

"When will you see the diary?"

"I'm leaving the money—."

I interrupted. "You're leaving the money? How much? Will you see the diary or just leave the money?"

"Twenty-five thousand," Charlie said.

"*Only* twenty-five?"

"It's all I'm willing to give him. "

"Why give him anything without the diary?"

"I didn't have a choice."

I kept shaking my head.

"Don't worry," he said. "It's only money. Think of it as a sales deal. Give a little, get a lot. We'll know soon if he has the diary or not." His cheeks flattened and he sobered up. "Nora and I are together on this. I'll pick you up at five fifteen," he said. "Be ready."

"Just don't oversleep."

"Don't worry. This is the last appointment I'd miss," he said, and then he kissed me, leaving a burning whiskey smudge on my cheek.

At midnight, our three Tibetan Buddhist workers lit a bundle of firecrackers and shot off bottle rocket rainbows and fountains of sparks. They showered across the sky then vanished like stars crossing the moonless February night.

As we watched and cheered the fireworks from the front porch, the freezing night air seeped into our sweaty clothes. Huddled together, tangled in tribal palhood, we sought warmth in each other's folds and angles.

One of the women crooned a caricature rendition of 'Soy to the World' anthem until everyone joined in. Soon, a boisterous choir harmonized to the Christmas melody.

Soy to the World, the beans have come.
Let earth receive her seed.
Let e-ver-y hear-ar-arth prepare its pots and pans
For tofu and tempeh
For soymilk and agé
Let heaven and nature sing Let A T and nature sing
Heaven and heaven and American Tofu sing

Then, party energy transported the song into howling cheers of uninhibited release and I slipped down the side porch stairs to my car.

Exhausted from the tension, the cooking, the party, dreading what I'd have to go through with Charlie and Benko in the morning, I climbed into my car. I heard Charlie bellowing "Happy New Year" to the workers as they wobbled around his wide Victorian porch. If the deal he'd made with Benko didn't work out, Charlie would have to change his anthem and everyone at the plant would be singing "Oy to the World."

As I pulled out of the driveway into the street, the employee chorus gathered for another chorus of "Soy to the World." A police cruiser pulled up and double-parked. I stopped to watch. The Chief got out and walked to the porch with a smile on his face. The employee chorus faltered for a minute then, when Charlie waved his arms like a conductor, they burst into the refrain one more time.

Buhrman walked up the porch steps, wagging his head back and forth. Charlie greeted him in the same effusive spirit he'd displayed all night.

He and Buhrman talked for a minute then Charlie turned to the crew. He shouted, "Now, that's a party, folks. When the Chief himself comes out to complain, you know it's a party." Charlie lowered his voice and semi-slurred. "Chief was wondering how all you happy people were getting home tonight. Told him don't worry. Didn't he know about the shuttles?"

Like a tipsy magician, Charlie swung his arm around toward the street. A caravan of a dozen vans and taxis crawled down the street toward his house. Charlie stepped onto the sidewalk and waved. In unison, lights flashed and the cars slowed down. Charlie bowed to the singers on the porch.

"Step right up, folks," he said. "Door to door delivery for the greatest tofu makers in the world."

I watched the laughing crew stumble toward the vans' open doors as I drove off in the opposite direction.

After I'd locked my apartment door behind me, I got a glass of water and went into the living room to sit and relax a minute before I dropped into bed.

"Hello, Genevieve."

Benko's voice rumbled out of the shadows. I leapt out of the chair and switched on the floor lamp. He sat a few feet away, on the couch, leaning back with his legs up, resting on the coffee table. He propped a half-empty bottle of vodka on his lap, holding it like a tumbler between his massive folded hands.

"Get out!" I growled at him, controlling my voice so I wouldn't wake Liam up. "Get out!" I hissed. "Right now! I'm calling the cops."

"Don't. It's not worth it," he said. "Take it easy. I'm your friend."

"Benko. You're a bastard. You're nobody's friend. You're drunk." I started for the phone. As if in slow motion, he glided off the couch and grabbed me by my belt. I gasped and swung my arm around to hit him.

He laughed and pushed me onto the couch. "Relax. Easy as a baby bottom. I'm not hurting you. Everything Charlie and I worked out." He sipped the vodka, then tilted the bottle toward me.

I glowered at him.

He shrugged and pulled at the bottle again. "It's win-win, Genevieve." His demon eyes gleamed.

"What do you want?"

"That's it. You know," he said, grinning, his words dripping from his mouth in bitter clusters. "You want it, too. Admit it. Let yourself. Smell it, sweet flower smell. Your breath. At the party we talked so nice."

"I'm giving you one minute then I'm screaming."

"Wake up Liam? He needs sleep. He has swim meet tomorrow?" His voice resonated between real menace and fake concern. I had to get him out, fast.

"One last time, Genevieve. Unforgettable one more time. Nobody will know. I go away and you remember me."

I glared. I wanted to try to cajole him but I couldn't control my reaction. Panic was climbing my back. Breathing deep, hard, I readied myself to launch the most blood-curdling yell I could.

"My beautiful long-haired redhead. You're so tall and fine. Perfect hourglass shape. All men want that. Liam's fine. A good looking boy. Smart. Friendly, like his mom. He's safe. His bedroom door is shut. He sleeps deep, I know. Him nothing bothers."

I screamed. His hand came down on my face like a hard pillow. I kicked and bit at his fingers and clawed at his face. He held me easily, pinning me down but letting me breathe. He smiled almost wistfully. His calm horrified me.

"Liam's fine," he said again. "Be quiet? I'll show you."

I nodded. He raised me, and with his palm loosely covering the lower half of my face, he walked me to Liam's room. Cracking the door, he let the living room light shine on Liam's bed. My son lay on his back, his arms and legs splayed out of his covers, his face all dreamy.

Relieved, I sagged against Benko, but immediately bolted up straight as I felt his pelvis slide and rub against my hip.

He closed the door quietly and spun me back toward the living room. "Will you be quiet if I let go?"

I nodded my head vigorously, scraping my nose against his callused fingers.

We sat down on the couch, side by side. He retrieved his bottle and gulped. I couldn't move or say a thing.

"I'm sad, tofu queen," he slurred. "Beautiful loving, eating together. My sausage once upon a time you never got full. You don't want me now. Makes me sad."

"Benko, please go. If you go now, I won't say anything to anyone."

"It's problem like everything now. All a problem. I hoped we could tell everyone we love each other how much you can't count. Like silo of full of beans." He snorted and coughed. "Maybe we marry? Liam likes me. You know." His head dropped onto his chest. He seemed to fall asleep. "You could have saved me," he mumbled.

"Too late. Way too much has happened."

Adrenaline poured through my body and mind. How could I convince him to go? He could control me physically, so the only power I had was words.

He straightened up and moved his face close to mine. His vodka breath stank. "Too late. Yes. The light. Too bright."

He leaned away and reached up, easing the table lamp's rheostat down until we sat in shadow. The room was so hushed I heard the second hand from my armoire clock skidding click by click into the past. Benko's body shuddered and slumped, his head fell back onto the couch and the bottle slipped from his hand. I let it fall and watched vodka dribble out onto my carpet. A snort erupted from his nostrils.

Afraid to disturb him, I sat for a long time, exhausted from our encounters already that night. I extricated myself slowly, hoping I could get to Liam and escape with him before Benko startled awake. I began to stand up and his arm clutched mine and I fell back. Rigid, I banged into his side.

"See," he said, "how our bodies fit so nice? Bolt and nut in factory we say."

He let me go and bent over to pick up his bottle. He poured the dregs into his mouth and mumbled, "Now I'm going. See how nice I am?"

He lurched to his feet. "All worked out. His bargain if Charlie keeps, win-win. Happy?"

If he was leaving, my best strategy was to stay quiet. He went to the kitchen sink and turned on the tap. Returning to the living room twilight with a glass of water, he signaled for me to stand up. "I'm not happy why? You know?" His voice cracked.

He drank and slammed the half-full glass onto the floor. The carpet's thick nap softened the fall and the glass bounced, unbroken. "This piss tastes water!"

I kept myself still as a rabbit caught in headlights. Totally at the mercy of whatever alcoholic mood possessed him, I was afraid that any response now would provoke his rage, but his melancholy calm returned.

"No. No. Truth? I miss you." He stumbled around the room, bumping into chairs, finally bracing his back against the wall. "One time sausage you couldn't keep hands off, yes? Now lost." He laughed. "Not even one more time. Tonight no chance. That's problem with vodka. After two liters, all you do is sleep. Used to take four. I'm getting old."

"Why don't you go home and sleep it off."

"I came to say good-bye."

"All right." I said. "Let's good-bye on the porch," I said, tugging at his sleeve. "You need some fresh air."

"I need more something. You," he said, putting his palm on my breast.

I winced and stepped back and he laughed again.

"Give me something to remember."

Whatever I could give him to get him out the door was fine with me.

"What about this necklace?" I said, starting to unfasten the clasp. "It's gold and it has a yin yang symbol. You can remember me and tofu."

"You keep your gold. I want something about you. More deep." I waited. His eyes widened as an idea came to him. "What color underpants tonight?"

"I don't know," I said. "I didn't notice when I put them on. Blue, I think."

"Let's see," he growled.

I lifted my crimson and emerald Chinese party skirt up as modestly as I could.

"God," he said.

"Yeah, blue," I said, dropping my dress.

"Blue sky. Like I feel flying with you. Let me have them."

"Will you leave?" I said, bargaining.

"Maybe. Yes. Give me. I'll go."

I started to slip out the underpants but he stopped me.

"Let me."

He sagged to the floor and fell against my knees. He straightened himself and ducked under the hem of my skirt. I kept my eyes closed as his whiskered jaws scraped the flesh on the inside of both my thighs. Leaning his head against my knees, he reached one hand up behind me under my skirt and yanked my pants down halfway. He jerked his head back and pushed them down to my ankles. I stood rigid, timy thighs clamped together.

"Help Gen. Gen, you have to."

I lifted one leg to step out of the pants. He pulled them out from under my shoe and jammed his head between my legs.

"Be nice," he muttered.

I wanted to slam my knee into his face, but I resisted and clenched my jaw as his warm tongue slid up my thigh. His two hands clutched my naked bottom and he pulled my pelvis into his face. His hot breath sent a flutter of pleasure into my stomach and then he began to lap at my clitoris. He probed and pushed and nibbled. He began to lick at my labia, sticking his tongue into me as far as he could.

I slapped at his head through my skirt. I clenched my thighs and he squeezed me tighter. With one hand, I reached around to try to peel his fingers off my bottom, but he'd sunk them into me so deep I couldn't pry them out.

With both hands, I hammered my palms onto the top of his head through my skirt. He didn't respond. I started to topple back so I opened my legs to get a foothold and regain my balance. He rammed his head into me and began vibrating his face back and forth, like a mechanical loofa sponge scraping my thighs and my labia.

I pounded and pushed his head. I pushed so hard, the waistband of my skirt tore and I slipped and fell backwards. My neck banged against the arm of the couch and he fell on top, pinning me. He lay across the lower half of my body, his head wrapped like a turban in my Chinese skirt, snoring.

My labia burned. Agony racked my head when I moved it but I had to get up. I wiggled and slithered out from under him. I rolled him over and began to creep toward Liam. I stopped to pick up the phone.

Benko's huge wrist grabbed me by the ankle.

"Don't go."

I struck at him with the phone, but he caught my arm.

"Be nice, Gen. I just want to show you love."

"I hate you. Get out."

"I'm drunk," he said, grunting. "We'd have great time." He held on to my arm and pulled himself up.

I backed away, but he pulled me toward him. His eyes closed and he fell against me again, drooping his head across my shoulder. I waited, wanting to let him fall into a deep sleep before I shoved him away and ran. I waited too long.

He raised his head, bringing his eyes to within a few inches of mine. "Good. You're still here." He blinked, struggling to stay awake. He gripped my forearm so tightly, my fingers went numb.

"I'm going now," he said. "You don't want me. I'm going." Without letting my hand go, he pointed to the floor. "Here. Pick up."

I saw my underpants hanging from the tip of a rocker arm on the rocking chair. I bent over and picked them up, depositing them on his broad palm. Slowly, he raised them to his face and inhaled deeply. He shivered and gasped like a dog splashed with cold water.

Dropping my arm, he grabbed me around the waist and bent into me. Slobbering a kiss on my face, he snickered.

"I kiss real good. Right? Nora taught American kissing. I like fucking her, but you. Over all them I take you."

He let me go and taking time to stuff the pants into his jacket pocket, he jerked open the door and backed out. His heel snagged the doormat and he stumbled to his knees. Coughing into his fist, he picked himself up and hobbled off the porch into the night.

I slammed and locked the door and shoved a chair under the handle. I ran to the back door, jamming another chair against it. I checked Liam again, examining every window lock, and went to the phone.

I called the police and told them I'd heard strange noises outside and would they send a patrol car into the neighborhood? I'd heard them before, I said. I was afraid.

I sat with the lights on, watching and listening. I prayed I'd seen the last of Benko for the night, but unless he'd passed out from drinking, I couldn't count on his staying away. After the third approach by the police cruiser, I lay down on the couch. I lay there with my eyes and ears wide open until I heard a car pull into the driveway.

I picked up the phone and went to the window and pulling the drapes apart, I peeked out. Freezing rain had smeared a coat of ice on everything. With his arms flung out for balance, Charlie worked his way up my ice-crusted sidewalk. He slipped from side to side, sliding along like a kid skating across a pond.

Chapter Five

Charlie

BECKY'S DIARY

*deep as midnight, wet
to my bones, i sink,
dive down, rise on swelling waves*

The morning after the Year of the Rooster party, I showed up right on schedule at Benko's house. Genevieve waited for me outside in my old nondescript Honda. I parked down the block, so she could watch the door from a fairly safe place.

If something strange happened, she'd call the police right away. If I came out and Benko didn't, everything was fine. If he came out and I didn't follow him within two minutes, she'd call the police.

"The whole thing should take five minutes. Keep the car running."

"I should come with you. He's probably drunk. When I came home last night, he was waiting for me. Drunk. He tried to rape me but he couldn't he was so lit."

"Jesus. Did you call the cops?"

"Yes. But I didn't say his name. Just I was scared somebody was stalking me."

"Good. He'll be inside then. Whatever you do, don't come inside," I said, counting on my own booze bravado to compensate for the bravery I'd left back in my bedroom.

I'd had a couple of shots of whiskey to chase away a bloom-ing hangover. I barely slept all night and I'd had three cups of coffee already so I wasn't worried the whiskey would make me too drunk to make the deal. I had ten thousand dollars in cash and a twenty-five thousand dollar bank money order. First, I'd give him the ten thousand in cash, show him the money order, and after I read the diary, I'd make it out to him. He'd get the rest later, when he handed over the book and any copies. And I was sure I had everything.

The money was a lot less than he wanted, but I gambled on his desperation to get out of town. Tried to rape Genevieve? He'd lost any edge he had over me.

His little house was set back from the road like most of the homes in the neighborhood. I scuffed up the slick driveway and knocked on his side door.

He growled, "Come. Come." He sounded impatient.

I walked into the dingy kitchen. The ceiling hung down less than a foot over my head and he'd drawn the shades down over the two small windows beside the sink. A low-wattage bulb glowed over a sink piled with pans and dishes. Benko sat at a round table in the middle of the room with a half-full amber glass in his big paw. His head bobbed and his eyes glazed.

I blurted out, "Where's the diary? I have the money."

Pie-eyed as I'd ever seen anyone, Gladonov grinned and raised the glass to me. "Come in. Sit down. Time to talk." His chin tilted down and he yanked it back. He smiled at me again. "I don't bite."

"Gladonov, I came to do business, not to argue with a drunk criminal about what belongs to me."

"Insult get you nowhere." He offered me a glass.

"I don't get drunk at sunrise, my friend. I don't need to be drunk to get through the day." Gladonov's attempt to distract me from our business raised my suspicions even further that I'd leave empty-handed, because he had nothing. A frisson of plea-sure rolled up my back: He was bluffing about the diary.

"You know, Mr. Big Man, you got one thing I want: money. You can have Nora."

The son of a bitch. "Leave Nora out of this, asshole. I worked my ass off for the money you're robbing."

"You worked? You slave driver. You're a good one, Charlie. Everybody thinks: Charlie honest and kind. I know you crock of shit."

"Benko, let's get this over with. Cut the lecture and give me the book. If you have it." My next move would be to turn around and head for the door.

"You're no better than anybody, Greer. You got money, that's all." He swallowed half the whiskey remaining in his glass, coughing a little. "Inherited from the wife? Good luck, eh? Now who's got the wife?" He laughed, coughing and hacking.

"Leave the wife out of it, I said. You fucked her. So what? You sneak around my back and fuck my wife. It means nothing in all this except you're a traitor. I did everything for you and all you want is to fuck the Greers."

He hefted himself up from the table and stumbled over to me. "Let's see cash."

His sour boozy breath nearly blew me over. Bloodshot eyes squinted out of his puffy face the color of a raw scab. He spread his legs to balance himself and leaning back, he clutched the table.

"Let's see the diary first. You know the condition."

"Fuck with me?"

He picked up a wrench from the table and gripped it hard. The veins in his arms bulged. His face reddened.

I opened my briefcase and pointed to the money.

He indicated that I should lay it on the table. "Count it," he said.

I counted out the bills, piling up ten stacks of ten hundreds on the floor of my open briefcase, and showed him the check, gritting my teeth to keep from chattering. "This is yours, too. Let me read the diary and I'll sign it over to you."

"Money order? Idiot. You don't have to sign it. All I do is write 'Tofu King Charles Greer.' Bank says 'Benko, take money.'" He laughed, grunting like a dog.

I backed away from the briefcase with the money order in my hand. "Show me the diary, Gladonov. Then you'll get the check."

"You crazy fuckin'. I want the money, I take it." He wagged his head back and forth, incredulous at my stupidity.

Without the booze in my gut driving out all my common sense, I'd drop the briefcase and split, but I stood glued to the floor, focused on taking the diary with me.

Without turning around, Benko reached behind his back to retrieve a half-full whiskey bottle. "Here, boss. Last chance. Drink with me. Celebrate. Laphroig. You bought it."

"I won't drink with you."

He had the wrench, he was crazy, I knew he'd take all the money as soon as he wanted but I had nothing to lose and I doubted he'd try to kill me. He might hurt me a little, but he was really only a con man who couldn't get it up any more.

Gladonov wagged the wrench up and down, as easy as shaking a fever thermometer. Watching my reaction, he swallowed the rest of his whiskey. "Where's all the money? I said fifty thousand right now. Fifty," he said in clear, simple American English. "Where is it? Don't make me mad."

"I told you, Benko. Give me the diary, I'll give you the whole hundred."

Considering his next move, he poured himself another glass of Laphroig and toasting me, he said, "Okay, boss. Hundred fifty, right?"

He wavered between amiable cooperation and angry threat. He wasn't sure whether I had all the money or not. We both had to keep our options open until we had a little more information about who had what to give.

"Diary, sure. I'll get it for you. Like always, no problem. You're the big boss. Honest Charlie. You give me fifty now. Hundred this afternoon."

He shuffled into the living room and fumbled in one of the stuffed chairs. When he came back holding a book, my knees wobbled.

She must have bought it in a supermarket. A mottled green-and-white school notebook lay across his hand like the Book of Revelations. I reached for it.

He pulled it back. "Wait. My fifty. Then you get the book."

"Jesus, Benko. I told you. Here's twenty-five now and the rest soon as I can. I can't have it for three weeks. We gotta wait for the customers to pay us."

"Shit tough. I'm in the air today. Gone. With all my money. I knew Charlie Greer would try to fuck me, like you did poor Becky." "Shut up, Gladonov. Take the thirty-five and get out."

"I need one more thing, Mister Tofu King."

"I don't have any more money. Ten dollars maybe." I reached into my pocket and eased out my wallet. "Here's twenty one dollars, all I have. Now give it to me."

He slapped the bills away. "You got something more. Your car." "My car?"

"LX. TofuMobile. Sixty, seventy thousand you paid? I'll take LX."

"You'll never get away with my car."

"Give me keys."

I backed away.

He shrugged. "No problem. Let's make it easy. Here. Read diary. Then you give me keys. You'll get down on your knees, beg me, take the keys, Benko. You give me whatever I want now. How about blowjob for book? You ask me, 'Take my wife, take anything.' Soon as I hand over Becky diary, its winwin. One hundred fifty, plus one car. Like I say, fair deal."

I grabbed the diary from his outstretched hand and opened it. "Sure. I'll read. If it's real, you get the keys. First I read the diary."

"Smart man." Benko slouched in his chair and slugged more scotch.

The diary entries were printed in round, childish letters. I'd never seen Becky's handwriting, but it could have been hers. The cover was scuffed, but the most terrifying and telling thing was its smell—Forest Rose, the perfume she always wore, and I always had to wash off before I came home.

"It's not hers. You bought this and wrote in it. I'm not giving you any thing."

Gladonov seemed to sober up. "No," he glared. "It's hers. No way I wrote it. You want the Chief to get it? That's all she wrote for Mister Tofu King."

I sat down at the table and opened the next page. Benko filled his glass and sat down across from me to watch.

"You don't think she wrote it? I guarantee it's hers."

"Your guarantee's worth a piece of used toilet paper."

He laughed.

Of course the diary was Becky's. As I smelled the perfume rising from the pages, her face appeared out of the gloom, smiling at me with those mischievous blue eyes. I listened, expecting her to crack a joke or giggle. She didn't, and her image faded and my eyes fell on the book. I forced myself to open it, and read.

Becky had written several notes on each page, dating each one and pasting a red heart beside several entries. She'd told me she stuck little heart stickers on anything she loved. I'd seen them on her kids' room door, on photos of her family and friends, on the dash of her car. She'd even tagged my bare chest with one. It was Becky's all right.

I squinted at the first page.

> apr 7 trying out a diary—my sister got one—said she learned so much about herself reading what she wrote—every night I'm supposed to write something—it's amazing she said—lets see how it goes

> apr 8 Bernie told me she has crush on new production manager—the Russian—good looking for sure—I told her be careful

    apr 14 Ralph called—drunk—I wasn't in mood for arguing—that's what always happens with him—i'm no good at writing—only wrote grocery lists and kids notes since high school

I thumbed ahead and started at what I read.

    may 20 Charlie looked at me again—I know what he's thinking—Me too—I like the way he walks—not much of a butt but he has long legs and the way his thighs bulge a little give me shivers—

    may 21 I told Bemie if Charlie ever came on to me I didn't know what to do—she said he's married—but what if he came on to me I said—I dont' know—play it by ear— He's cute she said he is cute—we've been looking at each other a lot—everybody's excited about being in the tofu movie—we're supposed to bring the kids in tomorrow—we came up with the idea at lunch one day to show AT as a family company

I flipped forward to the night we made love for the first time. No entry then, but two days later, she sealed my fate.

    jun 21 great company party other nite—so good I'm still messed up—not by beer or weed—Charlie—Charlie Greer the boss—the owner of the company and me—he brought me home & the kids weren't here & we fucked did it made beautiful love in my bed—he's sweet—I love his laugh—he never smoked hash before!—he said I don't want any bath salts or meth—I said don't be silly—I hate meth or stuff that makes you addict—he said ok I trust you—when he said that it made me shiver—trust   love!!!—I've never had a man who was so careful to make sure

I was happy and boy did he make me cum—about ten times!!!! at least !!!!—too bad he's married but o well—he didn't just fuck me, that's for sure!

The diary had to be real. Gladonov couldn't concoct this whole thing. The date of our lovemaking was too accurate. Why did Bernice say Becky didn't keep a diary? Maybe she never told Bernice about us. I hope not. Maybe nobody else knows. I shouldn't have told Nora and Gen.

"Good reading, Boss? Romance story, all women love romance," he mumbled. "You know, I'm best fuck they all had. Me, my giant prick. Nora must have told you about it. We did it five times a night. She wears me out. 'Benko's magic wand,' she calls it."

"Shut up, asshole. I don't care who you fucked or how big your flabby dick is."

"Genevieve. Oh her. I love her. I can't count the times she came every time I did her. Never had better piece in my life."

His narcissism showed me a weak spot. "Tell you what, Benko. This might be the real thing."

"S'real," he slurred. "I found it af' she died. Before cops came. Under bed. Idiot cops."

His stared at me cock-eyed as only a drunk can, then his head swung toward the side of the room across from the sink. His monitor and keyboard sat on a low table, propped up on an empty plastic shipping crate. The production office scanner perched on top of the monitor.

"You brought the scanner home?" I knew why.

He grinned but didn't reply. I understood immediately that my worst fear might come true: even if he sold me the book and disappeared, who knows who he emailed a copy of the diary to?

So far, I could explain the diary entry as her fantasy. After all, when I came home that night, Nora was sound asleep and I'd told her that I was home by midnight, a few minutes after I dropped off our inebriated employees at their homes.

I paged ahead in the diary and stopped at an early July entry.

jul 12 Benko stopped me in the locker room—he asked me to have coffee & I said no—Then he said he wanted to show me something—Come to his house—I said no—I told him not to but he came to mine—unzipped his pants—he has the biggest henry—we did it—he didn't come & neither did I—won't tell Bemie about him—she'd get furious—she already knows about Charlie—she thinks I should play my cards and not be an idiot—that means sleep with Charlie and wait for him to get a divorce—sure

july 25 I told Benko to leave me alone—I'm gonna file a sex hairassment case if he keeps coming on—

jly 31 I did it with Benko once more—last time—even if I like it, next time he tries, It's LAWYER time—I told Bemie and she knows a good one—only thing is if Charlie found out, I'm sure he'd never see me again—Charlie's why I don't go to the lawyer right now—he'd dump me and what else? he'd have to fire me and Benko—then what?

I raised my eyes. Gladonov's chin bobbed against his chest. He snorted a few times as if he were in a deep sleep.

"She hated you, Gladonov. She was gonna file a sexual harassment suit. She didn't because she was afraid I'd find out."

His head down, he muttered, "Fucked her good. Gave her good job. Her kids like me. Not like you, big boss. Money. She fucked your money."

I had what I needed now. I should have left but I couldn't stop reading. I flipped ahead to the last entry halfway through the book.

aug 19 guess what?—I can't believe it—I'm P-G!—I hope it's Charlie's—Bemie says get rid of it—I'll wait and see how I feel in a few weeks—who knows, maybe if it's

*Charlie's, me and him will get married—he's almost good
as divorced*

I knew it. She acted so strange when we did it the night before she died. A loopy grin curling her lips, she squirmed when she whispered, "Don't use a rubber tonight, Charlie. Anything that's gonna happen already did. We don't have to worry."

My denial firewall kicked in and I didn't go there. Not about to deal with anything scary, so I used the rubber. I'm sure I used a rubber that first night, too. I had to. Why didn't she tell me that night. Oh, I get it. That's it: It was going to be her hobbit's birthday present.

aug 22 Bernie says maybe the baby is Benko's—I took a PG test but it can't say how old baby is—could be his—shit—I'm gonna have to get rid of it—unless Charlie wants to keep it

aug 26 thinking seriously about this. If Charlie and me get married, I don't care if his wife gets half his money—by law, that's all she gets—I love him—does he love me???? I think so. He said it once and the way he holds me is definitely more than just sex.

aug 31 birthday party tonight—Bar B Q for the Big 3-0— Charlie's coming over after!—I told everybody the party's over at 9—I need time to get ready for work—sober up :-) Charlie has a present for me & do I have present for him—What's he gonna say when he hears I'm P-G???—I'm sure it's his baby—it's gotta be—I want to keep it—anyway— Happy Birthday to me!

That's it. This diary's going into the furnace, or I'm going to hell in a handbasket. I stuffed the book into my briefcase and stared hard at Benko. He snored. If he wasn't deep asleep, he seemed so drowsy I thought I could escape with it before he managed to get out the door.

Hurry up. Take the book and run. Get going. He might have a gun.

In case he heard me leaving. I wanted something to throw at him, to slow him down. I saw the whiskey bottle on the counter. I glanced at Gladonov as he snorted again and raised his head. His eyes were so glazed, I didn't know if he could focus, but he started to get up. I had to take a chance. I stood up and turned around, taking two quick steps to the counter and reached for the bottle. I clutched it by the neck and tensed to turn and aim it.

I swung around with the bottle in my raised arm in case he'd heard me. He had. Benko stood up and charged around the table, lifting his wrench. I tipped the briefcase over in front of him, spilling the bills and the diary onto the floor. He kicked it aside and, before I could hit him, he lashed at me, just missing my head. I smelled the grease on the wrench as it whooshed past my nose.

He regained his balance and stood there, the wrench raised behind his head. "You killed her, Charlie. I know."

"You don't know shit, Benko."

"You," he mumbled and the wrench drooped a little, then he woke up, sober as I'd ever seen him. "You fucker Charlie. You dumped Becky in my bean tank so cops think I did it. You didn't want that little baby, did you?" He sniggered. "She had my baby. She wants you, *Mister Money King*, to marry her. Not me."

He spit at me. Missed.

"You don't know shit. I slipped and she fell."

Goddam it. What am I saying?

"I had nothing to do with it." I was breathing hard. "It wasn't my baby. Was it yours? You raped her and knocked her up. Don't try to blame me for anything."

Benko's nostrils flared and his lips bulged, then his head rolled back.

He's drunk as a skunk. Do what you want with this piece of junk.

Now was my chance to turn the tables on him. "You sound like you know something. You know too much. You killed her. You hit her on the head and stuffed her in the bean vat."

He stepped closer. "That's what you want them to think. I know, ever since I called you at home. Waiting for me to call, eh? Clever as a rat. Mother fucker." He raised the wrench and lunged, slashing at me again, this time catching me on the chest and left shoulder, knocking me back but I stayed on my feet. Maybe the booze made him weaker than I thought.

He raised the wrench and I slammed head-first into his exposed chest. We crashed to the floor, two drunken sleep-deprived, raging animals. I felt I had the advantage because my whole body filled with hate. In reality, he had the upper hand and he showed it to me with a blow across the back of my head with his fist.

I lost consciousness. I came to with his fetid breath in my face and his hands digging in my pockets.

"Keys. Give me the keys."

I struggled to sit up. He shoved me back down.

"Give me keys. Shut up. Be quiet. Your kids. You want happy kids? Give me LX keys."

One of his gargantuan hands closed around my throat and squeezed my larynx and spine together. I started to swallow my Adams's apple. Pain drove my head against the floor while I kicked and pried helplessly at his fingers.

Gasping and pitching my head back and forth, I saw the kitchen door open and Genevieve flash into the room. Benko pounded his fist into my stomach. My body bent and I almost puked into his face.

"Benko. Get off him!" Genevieve ran over to us and started beating Gladonov on the back with her fists.

I called out, "Go away. Get out of here."

Gladonov swung his arm back, blocking her blows. He stood up and turned around, catching her by the hair. "Cunt."

She kicked at him. He slapped her on the head. She buckled and staggered. The fight went out of her.

"Charlie first. Then, I'll fuck you. Good. You'll come twenty times." He pushed her in the shoulder and she stumbled backwards, banging her head on the refrigerator. Then he turned back to me.

"Stop it, Benko," I groaned. "You have the money. Just go."

"LX keys." He shoved me down again and knelt on my chest to finish frisking me.

I tried to call to Genevieve, to tell her to give him the keys. We could let him go, I had the diary, but his knee had driven the wind out of me so I couldn't speak.

Genevieve pushed herself away from the fridge and picked up the whiskey bottle Benko had knocked out of my hands. She raised it in both hands over her head and with a crimson bulging face, she hammered it down on Gladonov's skull.

He collapsed onto my face, nearly smothering me. I jerked away trying to catch my breath. I turned and thrust as hard as I could and finally pushed him off into a puddle of glass shards and smoky scotch. A long splinter of glass sparkled from the top of his head like an icicle.

Gen and I sat on the floor, hyperventilating. We couldn't move. Finally, she whispered, "Is he dead?"

I crawled over to his face and put my fingers under his nose. I felt his moist breath.

"No."

"Check his pulse."

I lay my fingers against his neck. A slow pulse beat through his carotid artery.

He must be fakin', his eyelids're shakin'.

"He's alive."

"What now?"

"I don't know. Should we call the cops?

"Let's just get out of here," Gen said. "They'll think he had a brawl with some drunk friends."

I started to come to my senses. I noticed the diary in the shadow under the table. Gen didn't know I had it but Benko knew.

"What if he tells them it was us? We don't have an alibi."
"We could say we left town early to go on sales calls?"
"Sure," I groaned. "Perfect alibi."
She stared down at him. "Maybe he'll die."
"We'd be so lucky," I said.
"I don't want to kill him. I couldn't take that."
We stood up and brushed glass and spatters of blood and scotch off our jackets. We stared at him, our terrifying adversary reduced to a pile of sodden rags and sagging flesh. He lay with his prehensile hands folded over his crotch the way a child sleeps holding his genitals.

"We can't let him tell the police it was us. Buhrman will figure some way to arrest us. He'll charge us with at least assault and battery with a weapon. Maybe worse." Her face stiffened. "Did you get the diary?" she asked.

Should I let her in on the whole story? What good would that do? If she read the diary, she'd know about the baby. If anybody finds out about the baby, they'll put two and two together and think I killed Becky on purpose. "Uh, no. No diary. It was bullshit. He wanted the money and my new car. Like you said, it was bullshit blackmail. When I wouldn't give him the keys—you had 'em in the car. He came at me with his wrench."

"He's good with his tools," she said.
"Don't be funny. He tried to kill me."
"Funny? Don't be stupid." she said.
"We have to get rid of him," I said, looking around for something to give me an idea.
"Yeah. Easy to say."
"Throw him in the river? If we sink him under the ice, nobody would find him till spring."
She raised her eyebrows. "Jesus, Charlie. He's still alive. What if he comes to?"
"Yeah," I said, disappointed. "They'd find him."
"Yeah," she said. "We can't let anybody find out it's us."

"Another fucking investigation? More Enquirer? We lost Meng from the last one. What if we lose Giordano? We'll lose everything."

When I said "Giordano," her eyes fell.

"Maybe we could bury him?" I said half-seriously.

She turned back, pained, her shoulders bent inward and her face pale. "Alive? Charlie, listen to yourself. What are you saying?" "The ground's too frozen anyway."

Gladonov stirred and we jumped. His body spasmed for what seemed like thirty seconds. Glass shards fell off his shirt, his head lifted up and his eyes opened.

We gasped. Then, his head dropped and everything went quiet. "Check him," Genevieve said. "Did he die?"

I checked and felt his chest rising and falling. His breathing was regular but shallow. I was amazed at how little blood seeped out of his head. The glass must have barely penetrated the skull. He was probably just unconscious from Gen's crack on his head and passed out from all the booze he'd drunk since yesterday. If he came to, he'd probably attack like a wounded bear.

"Whatever we do, we better think fast. He might wake all the way up."

"I can't think. I laid on the couch all night worrying about him coming to kill me or Liam. Now this nightmare."

I stepped across Gladonov's body and bent down. He reeked of alcohol and garlic. Gen had dosed the Dragon Stew with garlic for the Rooster party.

If we didn't make Benko disappear, I doubted any of us would survive. Nora and the kids would never recover. They'd live in misery and shame and poverty. All because of one asshole with a prick bigger than his brain. I noticed the blood had stopped leaking out of the wound.

"Gen, at least we have to tie him up. If he wakes up ... Go find a rope or chain or something. He's gotta have some."

"What good will that do?"

"I don't know," I said. "Give us time to think?"

Slowly, she dragged her feet but found the door to the hallway. I heard her snap the light on and go into the back room. "Ow. Shit," she said. "Tools everywhere."

I knelt down and crawled under the table, retrieving the diary and stuffing it into my briefcase. Then I sidled over to Gladonov and put my hand on his forehead. It was sopping wet from our fight. I slid my hand down over his nose and mouth. Should I? If I smothered him now, no one would know. I pressed down. His head jerked.

I snatched my hand away and sat back on my thighs. No. I couldn't do it, not on purpose. I'm no killer, I don't care what kind of psycho he is. I'll take the diary and money and get out. We were never here. As long as I have the diary, he couldn't prove anything.

I'd have to take his computer and scanner. Christ, would this never end?

We were back where we started, but now, with the diary in my hands, I was in at least a litte more in control.

I watched him and sighed. We'd tie him up and get out and then wait. I'd check on him later. I propped my arm on the table and levered myself up. I turned to find Gen and get out of there when Benko groaned and grunted, an urgent wheezing. His legs bent at the knees and shot straight out. His body quaked, bouncing up and down.

I knelt back down and grabbed his chin in one hand, felt around the floor with the other for something to stick between his lips to stop him from biting his tongue.

His arm flopped and he reached up, clutching at my hand, trying to peel my fingers off. Then his legs dropped to the floor with a thud. A rill of trembles flooded his body, it jerked and quieted, oscillated again and went still. His arm sagged and his hand splayed palm-up big as a dinner plate beside my knee. He hadn't opened his eyes since he went down.

Genevieve's voice came from the hall doorway to the kitchen. "I've got an extension cord. Will that work?" then, from beside the body she said, "Charlie, what are you doing?"

I held out my hand to her and she tugged me up and I stepped back from the body. "Checking his breathing. He's gone. He must have had a heart attack or something."

She stared at me, then at him. Her eyes narrowed.

"He started jerking again. Kicking and shaking his head. A fit. Epilepsy or something. He pissed himself."

She hunkered down beside the body and, grimacing, she passed her hand in front of his nose. She held her fingers there for a long minute. She felt for a pulse in his neck. She felt for it on the other side. Then she laid her head on his chest while shot a narrow look at me. Her eyes glazed and she closed them, listening. Eventually, she reached out for my hand for help in getting up. I pulled her to her knees and held on to her hand.

She knelt beside the body, shaking her head. She gripped my hand, digging her fingernails into my wrist.

"O my God," she said. "I killed him."

I knew it already.

"Check him again," she said.

I knelt on one knee and put my ear on his chest. His green flannel shirt stank of sweat and grease and a harsh stink of urine underscored his helplessness. He lay totally still. Now what?

I slumped down beside Benko and let tears of shock or relief flow. Gen watched me coldly and she didn't try to comfort me and she didn't cry. When I stopped and wiped my eyes, I felt wide awake. She squatted across from me, with one hand on Gladonov's back, her eyes now closed, rocking her whole body on her ankles.

I picked myself up and circled around his body. I pulled her up by her shoulders. When she was fully up, we leaned into each other and moaned and whimpered.

She had trouble catching her breath but she didn't cry. "I didn't mean to. He was on top of you and I didn't know how to get him off. He's so strong."

I tried to comfort her. "It's all right."

"It's not all right. He's dead."

"I mean you didn't kill him."

"Oh, Charlie. He's dead. I hit him with a bottle and smashed glass into his brain. That's why died. If he really had a seizure, I gave it to him."

I held her against me as tight as I could. She didn't believe me that he had a seizure. She hit him and saved my life and I wouldn't let her think she killed him. Or she could think what she wanted but I wouldn't say anything about it. He was dead and the truth was, in one way, we both killed him. I didn't do anything that would make him end up dead. But I was in this all the way with Genevieve.

The kitchen was still dim but I noticed the sky beginning to gray outside the living room window. We had to get moving. We let go other each other and stared at the body.

"We gotta agree on something," I said. "He can still fuck our lives. We gotta get rid of the body and it's getting light out."

"I know. Where?"

"Maybe we can throw him in the lagoon behind the factory and he'll rot," I said.

"He'll float. Somebody will see him."

"So what? He fell in when he was drunk."

"If they drag him out, they'll see the gash on the back of his skull."

"Shit."

Another useless idea. We couldn't get rid of him underground, we didn't have a good place to give him a water burial. Staring down at the corpse, we let our brains whirl, trying to make sense out of the utter chaos of the last half hour. The universe was starting over again and we had to do something pretty amazing to make sure this latest Big Bang didn't blow us to oblivion.

My mind slowed, no thoughts, no Jiminy voice, no ideas. I wanted to drop to the floor and fall asleep. Fatigue washed through me and I didn't care if Buhrman walked in.

After a moment, Gen said, "This may sound stupid, but, what about the okara tank?"

"You mean throw him in?"

It was brilliant. She was brilliant. Pitch him in, let the oka-ra, the day's soybean waste cover him. Then in the course of the day, we'd ship him off to the hog farm we called Hog Heaven where the boars and sows would enjoy a gourmet Russian dessert.

Nobody ever checked inside the rail car, except Gladonov now and then when he needed to see whether he should move another car into place.

"Yeah," I agreed, adrenalized. Sober and sharp. "Sure. Let's do it."

"Wait a minute. Are you sure? What about his shoes?"

"Those hogs? They eat anything."

"Won't the farmers see him?"

"No way. One farmer for two thousand massive hogs. They dump the whole rail car on a moving trough. Everything's automatic. The hogs'll scarf him up before any human comes around. I've seen them devour a whole rail car of okara in half an hour."

"All right. Let's go. You take his head and I'll take his feet?"

"No way. I got him.

"You sure."

"Yeah. Don't worry."

I was about to do almost the same thing with Benko's dead body I did with Becky's—bury him in beans. Only Becky's were fresh and Benko's were ground up, the leftover lees of beans. Like Benko himself. A used-up husk of a man. The dregs.

Chapter Six

Charlie

THE BURIAL PLOT

overhead, frozen branches
rattle the trillion notes of
light, a winter choir

I gathered up the hundred dollar bills scattered around his kitchen and I jammed everything into my case along with the diary. I don't think I got all the bills, but I would come back and clean up later. Then I plucked the slightly curved four-inch blade of glass from the top of Gladonov's head.

I wiggled it and it slipped out like a knife out of Jell-O, clean except for a smear of blood. Thick red fluid gushed out of the wound for a few seconds, soaking his blond hair so I put my finger on the cut to staunch it. The skull felt soft and, when I removed my finger, the juice continued to seep.

Gen handed me a kitchen towel and I wrapped it around the head and wiped my hand on his shirt and lifted him onto my shoulders. I hoped the blood didn't spill on my clothes. I'd burn them anyway.

Staggering under his weight, but feeling the kind of strength a life-and-death situation fires your muscles with, I carried him to his car and lay him on the back seat. Checking the towel around his head for leakage and finding none, I slid back to the house. Gen was standing just inside with my brief-case. I reached for it.

"I'll take it, Charlie," Gen said. "You've got enough to carry. I'll put it in your car and you can get it later."

"That's good. Let me have my briefcase." I said. "I have a knife. Might need it to cut something."

She gave me the briefcase. I found the knife and shut the case. She reached for it. "That's all right. I'll take it."

She shrugged and walked slowly down the driveway to my car to drive it to her house where she would leave it for me to pick up when I was done with Benko.

After she changed her clothes, she'd leave town in her car, stop in to some of our customers' grocery stores along the way and talk to the managers, then she'd meet me later. In the meantime, I'd take care of what I had to do, drive Gladonov's car back to his house, walk home to pick up the Tofumobile and head out of town in the other direction.

By the time I left Gladonov's driveway, it was almost six and the gray sky had started fading to white. Looked like it would be a beautiful day.

Holding my breath and steering carefully on the slippery road, I drove the two miles to the factory in six minutes and parked at the rear of the building, out of sight from the street.

Nobody here. Damn lucky, Greer.

Because of the company party the night before, we'd scheduled the morning shift to start at ten, which meant that the first person wouldn't arrive at the factory until eight. I had two hours.

The parking lot was iced over so when I tried carrying his body to the rail line at the rear of the building, I staggered and slipped, falling flat on my back with Gladonov in my lap.

Risking a trail in the ice, I decided to slide the body across the slicked asphalt to the okara car. I hoped the sun or the warming air would melt the ice. If not, I only had a few minutes, so too bad about the trail.

I grabbed his ankles and dragged him to the railroad tracks. I stood over him, panting a dense cloud of breath around my head that seemed to drift, not rise. The mist blurred my vision for a moment while I considered my next step. One mistake now and after a whole year of dodging the Chief, I'd take a fatal dive.

I decided I'd better not trust the hogs to eat Benko's clothes. When I imagined the body cruising along the feed conveyor in Hog Heaven, I saw a riot of three hundred pound carnivores snuffling and snorting and ripping at the flesh, but ignoring the cloth.

No one would discover the corpse unless the hogs missed a knuckle or a rib, which I doubted. After a steady vegetarian diet of soy, those porkers would relish the meat treat.

Squatting down, I untied Benko's boots and tugged them off. One rank blue sock, one black, typically mismatched by a drunk. I quickly unbuttoned his reeking green mechanic's shirt. Once I pulled it off and dragged his soaking t-shirt over his head, his chest and belly steamed, releasing his last vital heat.

When I tugged at the cuffs of his black trousers, they slipped off, revealing red boxer briefs that bulged in the middle. Feeling squeamish for the first time, I grabbed the shorts by their sides and yanked. His penis flopped free and wobbled, half-erect, a sparse vapor rising from it.

Holy shit. Never seen nothing like it.

I immediately understood the women's fascination for him. His was easily twice as long and wide as mine and blue veins circled the shaft sort of like spirals on a barber pole. I wouldn't want to carry around a shillelagh like that banging against my thigh with every step. I'd have to learn to walk in a whole new way.

I was tempted to grab it just to feel what it was like to have such a honker. I reached for it, but it seemed to quiver. I came to my senses and jerked back from his godawful legacy, then turned and tended to business.

I piled the clothes and boots in a heap beside the tracks. Bending over him, I slid my arms around his sides. In my hands, his flesh was dense and firm. Hard muscle.

I heaved him onto my back in a fireman's carry and started up the icy ladder to the open top. I gripped the icy rung with one hand, held his arms around my neck with the other and stepped up on the bottom rung. I promptly slipped, tearing my hand loose from the ice, dropped the body, and this time, I fell on top of him, slamming my forehead into his jaw and my knee into his belly.

The blow shocked me wider awake. Morning became luminous. The bare branches of the trees shimmered like velvet wrinkles in the pale sky. The okara car loomed over me, a vast rusty hearse waiting to convey another wasted life to its next station.

I pushed off the body, rolled away, and stuck my burning hands into my gloves. As puffs of my warm exhalations evaporated in front of my face, sunrays struck my breath-clouds, tinting them with pale rainbow sparkles. I smiled to myself as if I'd risen early just to watch the sun rise.

Leaving Benko on the tracks, I climbed up the ladder, kicking and stubbing patches of ice off the steel rungs, to reconnoiter. The sun worried at the morning haze, so I expected it to wipe out all traces of my having climbed the ladder and the tracks in the parking lot Benko's head and shoulders had scraped in the ice. Sunlight was a double-edged sword right then. I had to hurry.

You got a break, Jake.

Jiminy was back. Somehow it was comforting. I wasn't the only one in this.

Back on the ground, Benko lay in a sunbeam, his face serene and golden. I saw the corpse as a young man: handsome and alluring. The wrinkles had disappeared from his forehead and his mouth hung open as if he were singing an endless one-note song. The little cannon propped in his lap had lost its loft, but it maintained its aim as if hopeful of one last shot.

I bent and hoisted him up again and draped him across my back. Climbing about as fast as I could, I trudged up the rungs, slipping a little, taking forever. At the top, I leaned over and folded myself over the three-inch wide steel lip and, turning sideways, I twisted quickly and heaved.

He slid off my shoulder and fell six feet with his head down but once his legs followed his trunk, he somersaulted, landing on his back with his arms and legs sprawled across a beige cone of ice-coated okara.

When he hit, his body whoomped like a small bomb striking and he crashed through the frozen soy pulp, exploding it into shards of ice and clumps of okara and a cloud of rancid steam.

Sealed under a coat of slush and ice, the tofu production waste had fermented at one hundred twenty degrees, souring into tangy hog chow. Once Benko's body shattered the frosted crust and cold air coupled with the hot moist pulp, a cloud of steam billowed up, hiding Benko's body in a small fog bubble. Then it floated up and away from him, some of it dissipating into the air, some forming crystals on the walls of the rail car.

With filaments of steam rising around the inert body, it seemed to smolder. If I were superstitious, I'd say I was watching his soul take a slow exit. His sallow skin and tawny hair blended into the tan okara as if he'd already begun to dissolve into his elements. Even the eager devil in his crotch had given up its ghost and lay between his thighs shriveled as an old banana.

I propped my shins against the top rung of the ladder and rested. Benko, as a human being, had deserved a better life and a better death. Benko as the particular human being he was deserved nothing better than a violent ending and this humiliating burial in waste. Not one twinge of regret, remorse or guilt bothered me.

Better Benko than you, my friend. You're breathing, he's met his end.

If this worked, Benko would become my best friend.

My ex-best friend.

I waited for the body to sink out of sight under the surface. It settled a little, but didn't sink. It must have compressed the okara where it landed. If I climbed into the tank, I'd make such a mess of the surface that anybody checking the level of the okara would notice and wonder what had happened. If I didn't force his body all the way down into its temporary grave, anybody who happened to see into the rail car would see the body.

I let myself down into the car as gently as possible. Naturally, I sank to my crotch in the hot muck. Sucking at me like quicksand, the okara scalded my thighs and formed a mist around me, saturating my pants as I slogged through. Starting with the feet, I shoved the body down into the steaming pulp, burying it as deeply as my arms could reach.

I plodded through the soy muck to the other side of the car to reach the ladder and I dragged myself back up. When I climbed out, my coat and pants and shoes had gained half an inch of okara insulation. I was soaked and steaming in the morning light like a primeval swamp creature rising into his first sunrise.

My pants and jacket began to stiffen in the sub-freezing air. I shivered, remembering myself as a kid playing in mushy snow then scraping toward home stiff-legged for supper. I walked into brush beside the tracks and bounced and stamped and scraped off the loose okara. With a stick, I scraped my clothes down, and with Benko's gear in my arms, I slipped and slid across the parking lot, oddly lighthearted, to the building where I let myself in through the employee entry. I dropped Benko's clothes beside the door.

In the employees' lounge, I removed my pants and jacket I ran into my office and pulled on the spare pants and shirt I kept in the closet.

Back in the factory, I grabbed a parka from the hook beside the walk-in cooler. I hurried back outside, my feet cold and wet but warming up. Along the way, I stuffed my wet pants and coat into a plastic garbage bag along with Benko's stuff.

I didn't have time to burn them. If I took the clothes home to hide them, I'd risk Nora's finding them. Hauling them to the refuse area out back, I chucked the bag into the dumpster that was emptied daily at ten a.m. with fifty other trash bags from the previous day's production and unloaded into landfill before noon.

Easing myself into Benko's car seat, brushing the soles of my shoes off into the parking lot, I drove Benko's car back to his house.

I parked the car in his driveway and walked home in watery morning light, carrying my briefcase like a city commuter heading for the train, slipping several times and taking a pratfall on a pool of black ice lurking on the sidewalk.

I bounced up, adrenaline still coursing through my muscles. I wanted to run, but forced myself into the scout's pace, fifty steps jogging, fifty steps walking, counting to keep me distracted and aimed to my safe and cozy house fewer and fewer blocks ahead.

I showered, changed into my grey suit and tasseled black loafers, swallowed a cup of orange juice, and left the house in my camelhair overcoat, ready for customers, just as the kids and Nora started making noises in the bathrooms.

I noticed that the ice had melted off the street where the early traffic wore it thin. Grateful for the clear asphalt underfoot, I walked along in the car tracks toward Genevieve's neighborhood. Her car was gone when I climbed into the Honda, and backed out of Genevieve's driveway at 7:30, steering east, toward my alibi. A fit of anxiety struck me and I swerved around, driving back toward the plant. In my euphoria at getting rid of the body, I realized the danger I'd left myself exposed to: Benko's and my clothes into the company dumpster, leaving a confession right under Buhrman's nose.

I slapped my cheek a dozen times to punish myself for setting myself up again for my destruction. Two blocks from the factory, I turned the car around. The startup crew was paid a bonus to be obnoxiously punctual. No doubt they'd punch in ten minutes ahead of time, even while sobering up from the company bash. I couldn't risk having one of my employees see me digging around in the trash.

If anyone found Benko and called the cops, they'd search the plant's premises, for sure. Even though the Chief was much smarter than before Becky's death, the odds were in my favor that they wouldn't catch on to anything suspicious before the garbage truck hauled away State's evidence number two and number three, our clothes, with Benko's corpse being number one.

I thought of calling off production with the excuse that everyone deserved more time off. I could retrieve the clothes when the plant was vacated. But then the hog farm wouldn't get its scheduled load of feed and they'd call the morning shift supervisor. He'd have to check the car, see some strange pattern in the okara, and all hell would break loose.

I was confident that no production worker would check the rail car to see if it was full. That was Benko's job and when the okara rose high enough to ship out, an electric eye read the level and shifted the okara exhaust pipe to the next car. Benko's coffin car and one other would fill and ship out by early afternoon.

I had to handle the suspense for a few more hours. As I drove, I puzzled out my solution to Benko's scanning the diary into his computer. I knew Benko didn't have any great skills so he would use the basic techniques anybody would. I knew how to erase that from his hard drive, but he may have known more about computers than he let on. I was a fair hand at computer security, and I counted on being able to trace any emails he may have sent with the diary attached: the last loophole that could strangle me. I'd count on my IT guy to sterilize everything. I wasn't finished with Benko yet.

***

At two in the afternoon, Genevieve and I sat exhausted in a Starbucks in Albany, picking at crumbs of our muffins. We barely spoke while we ate. We'd each visited several supermarkets and seen customers to establish alibis.

I ordered another cappuccino and made a call. When I brought the coffee back to the table, I said, "It's over, Gen. I checked with the factory. The okara shipment left on schedule half an hour ago."

"Thank God," she said. "We're free."

"Not totally. We have to make sure no one saw the body at the hog farm. Four hours from now, poof. Pig poop."

She wrinkled her nose and grit her teeth. "All right," she said. "We have no choice."

"Don't worry. I'm not." She needed to see me confident and so did I. Play it till you lay it.

I watched the other customers chewing their rolls and slurping their lattes, prodding their torpid minds into a couple of hours of semi-alertness. The same thing I needed.

Genevieve covered my hand with her cool palm. "I believe you. Now, I have some more news."

"Good, I hope."

"It is. Really. You'll understand."

My blood sugar was so low, I was wrung-out and half-asleep, so whatever she reported, I barely cared.

"After my Hawaii trip, I'm leaving American Tofu."

I sat up. How could she leave now?

"I have a job that pays twice as much and it's a long way away from all this. I'm going to San Francisco," she said. "I want to raise Liam in a city, not this hick town. Anyway, after this morning, how could I stay at Tofu? I'd always be thinking about what happened."

"Yeah. I see that."

She's known it for a while. Strategy's her style.

In about two seconds I realized that she'd planned this. I didn't blame her. If we hadn't vanished Benko, he'd have made her life miserable. Now she'd be so traumatized, she'd be useless at work anyway. Not that it mattered. Her customers loved her so much she could only do right.

"I'm not surprised," I said, "only sad." I could barely croak loud enough for her to hear. When he choked me, Benko had burned his fingerprints into my neck. I expected to have to wear turtlenecks for a couple of days, and I couldn't let Nora or the kids see me without my shirt on. "I wouldn't mind leaving, too. But I gotta stay and forget about it. Honestly? I tell myself what happened had to happen. The world's better off without him. But how am I gonna build the company without you?"

"You'll hire somebody better."

"I'll miss you so bad." I squeezed her fingers. "Nora won't be able to get along one minute without you."

"I'm sad, too, but I have to go. You'll be fine."

"We'll be fine, especially when we hear the hogs enjoyed their gourmet lunch. I know you'll be fine, too. San Francisco. What will you be doing?"

"It's a good job. I'll tell you all about it, but now there's one thing we have to do."

She seemed to know she could ask me for anything, and right then, with the vision of the blade of glass jutting from Benko's skull fresh in my mind, she could. "Jesus, what now, Gen? I barely have enough energy to drink this coffee. Look at me. Half-dead myself."

"This is easy. No, hard, but we have to: Never talk about any of this again. Wipe it out of our minds. I can't stand thinking about him. The sound of that bottle smashing. It's the pigs that gross me out as much as anything." She pulled her coat tight and zipped it up. Steam condensed on the windows and it must have been eighty inside the Starbucks.

"Oh, not talk? Maybe that's best." If she was gone, it would be easy. That was another good reason for her to go. She was so smart.

She laid her hand on my cheek. "Let's go. I gotta go home and climb in bed and stay away from the shop. I'm sorry."

"Take tomorrow off," I said. "Nobody will think anything weird. Then you show up and announce your fantastic luck with a new job and pack your stuff and say good-bye to everybody. You can put up an act for a couple of weeks. Make a smooth transition. In pain, but normal. Everybody will understand. We're all gonna miss you."

"I'll try, Charlie. For you and Nora and Liam. I need some sleep now to help me get my spirit back. I still feel like a boiled wonton. I don't know if I'll ever be able to see a bottle of whiskey again without seeing his body flat on the floor."

"I'll miss you, Gen."

"I'll miss you, Charlie. You were a bastard sometimes, and an idiot, but you were real and I always loved you for not pretending to be somebody better."

"You know what?" I said, sitting up, embracing with my eyes this woman who I owed so much to. "You and me? We're closer now than most husbands and wives. It's wild how Benko finally brought us together."

"What do you mean? This is about as romantic as a compost bucket."

"I don't mean romantic. I mean we're closer than almost anyone can be. We'll never be the same because of him."

She pursed her lips and sat back. "Lots of people will never be the same."

"Not the way we will."

She nodded, "Yeah, it's true," and stirred her coffee.

"The worst thing about this?" she said. "I mean, except Becky died? The sad thing is we really do have to forget each other. I'm sorry. I can't get the sound of the bottle smashing out of my mind."

"It'll take time for that. I won't forget you. I could never forget you. After everything we've been through?"

"I don't mean really forget each other. Once I leave? Not see each other. Maybe never again."

She started crying dand I tried to smile reassurance. I offered her my napkin.

"Never say never. Long time, yeah, that's all right, but never?" I groaned. "I love you and I'll have to find out how you're doing?" How could I not love her after all we'd been through. Comrades-inarms. Captains in combat.

She leaned over and kissed me on the cheek and sat back and blew her nose.

We finished our cappuccinos and found our way to our cars. She had stopped at the Genesee Street P & C and talked to the produce manager, and I'd stop at a couple of Shop Rites and independent stores. In case anyone asked, we'd be covered. Plenty of witnesses observing us do our regular routine of customer visits.

We walked arm in arm across the parking lot. Before we separated, I said, "Meet me back in my office at five. I want to give you something."

"What about my day off? I don't know if I can last until five. I gotta sleep."

"Yeah, I forgot. No hurry, I just want to make you feel better. I'll call you tonight, say eight o'clock? Let you know if I hear anything. Any problems at the farm, we'll know for sure by then."

"All right. I'll be asleep so let it ring," she said. letting her head rest on my shoulder.

I leaned my cheek against her hair and closed my eyes. We could have fallen asleep standing right there.

After a few steps, I opened my eyes and lifted my head. Pulling her closer, I said, "I'm a little nervous. Something weird could always happen. I'm not too worried. But if they find him, we have nothing to do with it."

"I know. I've seen the way those hogs gorge themselves. I hope none of the farm hands are watching."

"Tiny chance of that."

"Right now, I'm so wiped out I can't think about it." We let go of each other and, after a long hug, she got into her car.

"Drive safe," I said. "Wait till you get home to fall asleep."

"Drink hot lemonade with fresh ginger. It works miracles for a hoarse throat." She sighed and rolled up her window and drove away.

Always thinking about others, that woman. Hot lemonade with ginger. I may have to try it if I don't get my voice back.

Chapter Seven

Charlie

FAIR SHARES

*I turned everything
over, upside down no
diary to be found*

That night, after drowsy, achy hours of driving around, staying out of sight, I trudged home to a quiet dinner with Nora and the kids.

"No diary," I said, as I sat down. "Everything's fine. He's gone. He took ten thousand and screamed at me and cursed and said he was leaving town. Didn't care what happened at the factory."

Tears streamed down Nora's smiling face. Chuckie scowled and Rissi said, "Mommy," and jumped out of her chair and ran to Nora.

"I'm fine, honey," Nora said. "Daddy told me good news, is all. Makes me happy."

Rissi pulled back and frowned at Nora. Then she smiled. "You're like Daddy now Mommy. He cries when he's happy, too."

I burst out laughing and Nora followed. The kids gave each other mocking faces, rolling their eyes, probably agreeing that their parents were crazy. After dinner, I said I had to go into the office for a while. I drove car to Benko's neighborhood and parked a block away. If that's what she did when she was hav-

ing her affair with him, maybe the neighbors were used to seeing the car.

I let myself into the house, found a broom and dustpan and
swept up all signs of the fight, dumping the glass into a bag I'd
throw into a trash bin at a rest area on the interstate. Benko's
blood had stained the brown carpet with a smudge as big as
a watermelon. I washed it as well as I could and prayed that
when it dried, it would blend into the nap like old ground-in
dirt. I stuffed the rags into the trash bag with the glass.

I found the nine hundred dollar bills that were missing from
the count I'd made earlier, then I started Benko's computer. Before I went to work, I activated my cell and called the hog farm.
Rare, but I'd checked on okara shipments in the past. Thank
God, the farmer had nothing to report. I called Genevieve.

***

"Gen. Sorry to wake you." "What?"
"All clear.
"What?"
"Go back to sleep." "Thanks. I thought so." "We're clear."
"Yeah. What time is it?" "Nine."
"Mmmm."
"See you in the morning?" "How about, after lunch?" "Sure."

***

By midnight, I'd cleaned Benko's hard drive of all evidence and
echoes of the diary. I printed out a list of Benko's few email
communications since August. He'd made all of them from the
factory since he didn't have an internet connection at home.
He'd sent a half dozen notes to Genevieve, bought several cases
of vodka and scotch on-line, downloaded some porn, joined a
dating website. It seemed the scanned diary was unmoved from
the hard drive, but I'd have to search all his emails. He must
have had a hard copy somewhere. I hoped not.

I checked the company cloud storage and found nothing personal for Benko, as expected. He'd told me once he didn't want to be traced every time he hit a key on the keyboard.

I returned the scanner to the production office at the factory and deposited Benko's computer with the other old office equipment in a storeroom in the company warehouse. I'd pour through his little office as soon as I could. I returned to Benko's house for one final inspection.

As far as I could tell, he managed his home like any bachelor drinker with dirty laundry strewn around the bedroom, an unmade bed, grimy dishes in the kitchen and on the coffee table in front of the TV, newspapers piled up.

Wearing gloves, I poked around under the bed, under the mattress, in the closet corners, every shelf and cupboard, even in the toilet tank. No copy of the diary. I went through the whole place a second time.

After thinking about it, I left the heat on and the door unlocked, and eased my way casually back to Nora's car and drove home.

Nora and I sat up for two hours, crying, laughing, holding each other. I told her that when I called Benko's bluff about the diary, he'd struck me with his wrench and run out of the house.

"I followed him, but he disappeared."

"Where could he go?" she wondered.

"Some woman's? Who cares. Soon as he comes in tomorrow, I'm firing him."

"What if he won't leave? What if he attacks you again?"

"I'll fire him in public, in the production room. The workers will protect me if he goes nuts."

"I'm still scared." Nora cuddled up and threw her legs across my lap, squeezing me as hard as she could.

"If he loses it, I'll call Buhrman. He needs to put his energy into something worthwhile." I tried to joke but Nora ignored me.

"C'mon. Let's go to bed," I said, more spent than ever in my life. "When he shows up, I'll give him his Chinese New Year bonus early and three months' severance. He'll be gone by noon. I'm not worried."

Way to cover your tracks, but don't think you can relax.

***

I arrived at the factory at 1:30, still groggy with a sleep debt hanging over me like a concrete cloud. Gen lay on my office couch with my grandmother's orange and green afghan pulled to her chin and her arm thrown over her eyes. I closed the door and tiptoed to my desk.

"You're late."

"Sorry. Slept late, then got tied up on the phone with production. Without Benko here, we had to make sure the schedule was set for the rest of the week."

Genevieve sat up and folded the afghan and lay it over the back of the couch. I switched on the lights.

"I need a lot of time off, maybe the rest of my life."

"Me, too. But everything's fine now. All we do is act normal."

"What's 'normal,' Charlie? How can anything be 'normal?'" She tossed aside the blanket and stood up and paced. I felt as bad as she did, I'm sure. Who wouldn't? But I was so relieved, I wanted to laugh and shout. If Benko hadn't bruised my chest and shoulders so badly, I would laugh.

I rose and put my arm around Genevieve, tugging her close. She sniffled into the tissue I offered her.

"Does Nora know anything?"

"No way."

"What about the factory workers?"

"They think he's still sleeping off his drunk or so hung over he can't get out of bed."

"Two days in bed?"

"Everyone at the party saw him staggering out the door barely able to keep his head up. It's as good a theory as any."

She held her breath. "The farm?"

"Business as usual. It's done, Gen. Life goes on." I smiled. "The hogs are happy."

She grimaced.

"Our future is wide open," I said. "We can relax."

"Relax? What's that?"

The ordeal had wasted Genevieve. Not only Benko's death, but the Chinese New Year road trip must have gutted all her reserves. "You don't need to mourn him," I said. "He was evil."

"Mourn him? Shit, Charlie. You don't know half."

"What d'ya mean?"

"Forget it," she said. "He's gone and too much of us went with him."

She hated him, I thought, but love's always buried somewhere inside fury. Once you taste passion, you can't resist it, no matter what shape it takes. Love, hate, grief. It's a lot better than feeling numb. We both sat down and I reached into my briefcase and pulled out my wallet.

"Don't take this wrong, Gen."

I opened my wallet and removed a one hundred thousand dollar bank draft and offered it to her. She didn't respond so I closed her fingers around the check. She tried to give it back but I wouldn't take it.

"It's money I set aside for emergencies," I said. "It makes me much happier to give it to you. You suffered plenty from him, too." Easy come, easy go, I thought. Thanks, Meng.

A tiny curve of smile trembled on her lips. She stared at me with moist green eyes. She finally folded the check but held it between her fingers like a card she didn't know whether to discard or bet. "This goes right into Liam's college account."

"Good. Anything you want to do with it. It's yours."

"You're sure?"

"Yes. It'll cost you plenty to move across country. Get yourself a nice place in San Francisco. Besides, money makes money."

"This is my Soy to the World sales bonus, right?"

"No. You'll get that when the customers pay their invoices. This is my personal appreciation. It has nothing to do with business." She unfolded the draft and stared at it. "I don't know. Are you paying me off? Was this the money you planned to give Benko?" "Genevieve. No. You can use the money."

"It feels scuzzy."

"It's yours. If you don't want to cash it for Liam, give it to some homeless shelter or something." She and I stared into each other's eyes for a long time. Behind me, my email pinged twice into the silence. I watched her make up her mind.

"Thank you," she said as she inserted the wrinkled draft into her wallet. "Tell Nora thank you."

"She doesn't know about it. If she did, she'd expect me to give it to you. You know that." My voice caught in my throat. The words scratched across my larynx and emerged barely above a whisper. "I'll tell her."

Genevieve stood up again and stepped around the coffee table to my chair. She squeezed my cheeks in both her hands and tilted my face up to hers. "You gonna be all right?"

"I never felt better."

I lay my head against her firm belly and let the tears flow. She brushed her fingers through my hair, her nails caressing my scalp the way my mother used to. I pressed my head against her hopelessly. When I finally won her, I lost her forever.

She goes, you stay on the home turf. You both get what you deserve.

A fantasy about Genevieve that I put aside two years ago floated to the surface of my sorrowing mind: If I were her one and only, my life's purpose would be met. We could never live together, but this feeling's not about marriage or family. I've known ever since she first applied for the job that she and I had a special destiny and it had nothing to do with romance.

Nora says that we have all kinds of soul mates, not romantic love partners. Genevieve and I are definitely soul mates. I'm sure I'll see her again. After she's settled and thriving in her new life, I bet she contacts me. If she doesn't, it won't be hard to find her.

***

On the third day of Benko's absence from work, I called Buhrman to let him know Gladonov hadn't come in to work since the Year of the Rooster party. If I waited any longer, he'd think I was hiding something. Once I told him, Buhrman went to Gladonov's apartment where he found Gladonov's car in the driveway and his apartment empty.

By then, I'd scoured every drawer, file folder, bookshelf, garbage can and box in his office. I turned everything over in his workshop. No copies of the diary anywhere. I didn't feel free yet, but my neck and jaw loosened up a bit. IT gave me the all clear. The headache I'd had for three days faded.

When Buhrman stopped into the factory to give me his latest news, I insisted that he put an all-out effort into finding Benko. I told him Gladonov had acted irrationally at the party and went home drunk. I needed him to run my factory and the least Buhrman could do now was help us find him. I had no idea where he went, but rumors had started to fly around the factory crew that he disappeared to escape suspicion that he was involved in Becky's death. I wanted Buhrman to think he'd found the hot trail of the elusive killer at last.

"What d'ya think we are, Charlie? New York City? You some kind of celebrity? I'm supposed to hire somebody just to go after him so you can make your toad food? Show me where that's in my budget. You've already cost this town plenty."

Buhrman almost drooled spite but the disappearance of one of his main suspects must have given him a sense of self-justification. He could give the D.A. a pretty good ending to the murder story.

Chief's a good cop, you gotta admit. But the bad guy's gonna come out on top.

I asked him, "My wife's nervous about Gladonov. So's Genevieve. Ever since Gladonov disappeared with her kid in Buffalo, she and my wife worry he might come back and they're afraid for the kids. How about posting a patrolman outside our houses until we're sure he's gone?"

He sputtered but without scorn. "Never heard of such a thing." "Just until we're sure he's gone."

"My overtime since last summer is more than your property taxes for a year, Greer. On your factory and that McMansion of yours. Sorry to say, but this town's gotta raise its taxes so guys like you pay their fair share."

Buhrman enjoyed playing the bumpkin, but he was so easy to see through. I wouldn't let him get under my skin any more. Besides, now we were negotiating the price of his special service.

He finally agreed to put a man on the factory premises and assign one to drive by my house and Genevieve's every half hour around the clock but, he said, if Gladonov showed up tomorrow after sleeping off a binge, the police department would send American Tofu the bill for every second his man spent on the case.

"What do you think about a hundred bucks an hour, Greer?" "Fine, Aaron. Whatever it takes to keep the kids safe and the mothers happy."

"Plus expenses."

"That would be donuts and coffee right?" I said.

Buhrman smiled and touched the bill of his cap and left, the humble, obliging civil servant.

Chapter Eight

Charlie

ASHES ASCENDING

by the icy stream, I
light the pages—
smoke drifts up, fades away

I burned the diary.

One afternoon, I loaded kindling and firewood into my LX and drove out to the river. I wanted to have my private ceremony, honoring Becky and closing this chaotic chapter of my life. I scraped a clearing in the snow with my boots and built a fire on the shore.

By now, I could almost recite the diary word for word, I'd read it fifty, a hundred times. If only she'd told me about the baby. Honestly, I don't know how I'd have reacted, but I know myself well enough to be sure I'd have done something honorable.

Standing close to the blaze so I could feel the heat on my calves and knees, and coughing in the smoke, I tore the diary apart, page by page, and set it on fire, offering it to the Buddha of good luck or whatever ironic god had mercy on me at the cost of two lives and who knows what other damage.

A wave of black burnt paper flowed toward my hand as a low orange flame followed it on each page, transforming the paper first into dark filigrees of ash then casting off white flakes into the rising air currents. They fluttered and bobbed and some of them brushed my hair and face and jacket like tatters of a shroud so fragile they disintegrated when they touched me.

The diary's cardboard covers guttered. Not wanting to leave any traces, I ripped them into pieces and while I bounced down the rough gravel road, I opened my window and sprinkling them little by little, I let them drift away.

For most of my life, I'd made denial my masterpiece. I was so good, I managed to turn my talent for denial outward and convince my wife, the Chief, my bankers, my customers, even my kids that I was who I was not. I did a beautiful job of convincing myself, too. While part of me played the role of the innocent, I willed the whole of me to believe it.

Perhaps being with Becky would have shown me the illusive real me. Becky, a simple woman who loved me, a simple man, and that might have been enough. Maybe she'd have died in an accident anyway. She had her fate.

You thought you were smart cuz you knew she was a tart.

Maybe if I'd been smarter about my motives, maybe if I'd given more to my marriage, maybe if ... aaah ... who knows?

I can handle more change than most people, and I don't regret risking everything to keep my family and my life intact. I did all I could to minimize the damage I'd done by falling for Becky and submitting to passion's reckless ultimatum: love or nothing. But where did I get the guts and brains to survive the Chief and Benko?

Underneath all my battling and tricking and deceiving had to be something like love, a desire for joy and connection, showing itself in other guises. The pure love I have for my kids, the responsible love I have for my employees, and yes, the married love I have for Nora.

Still, I have to admit, I loved myself more than any of them. The last thing I could do was live the rest of my life as infamous Charlie Greer, the guy who knocked up his employee and then she died by accident, ha, ha. Charlie Greer would not survive that.

Only you know who's to blame. What a shame.

As I neared town, my eyes dry in the cold breeze of the open window, I scattered the last pieces of the diary until all but a few were gone, each scrap taking the place of a tear falling.

Back in my office, I hid the remaining shreds in the lacquered box Meng gave me, concealing them inside the anaconda's jaw, my personal monument to love and ecstasy and survival. I locked the box in my desk expecting to feel closure or tangible release from my constant wariness, but trust in the way things were escaped me.

So I would go on, meeting whatever showed up next. That I could do this now, I was thankful for.

***

About a month after Benko sacrificed himself to the sausage lovers of America, Buhrman called. "I want to give you the update. My tentative final report before I back-drawer Gladenuff, least until we catch him in the flesh."

In response to my request that we talk now, he said, "No, I can't do it over the phone. Never know who's listening in. I'm going to a police chiefs' convention tomorrow, so let's handle it this afternoon. I'll be by quarter after one. Give you time for lunch."

He pulled up at exactly 1:15. I got in the patrol car with him.

"Security purposes," he'd replied when I asked him why we always had our meetings in the cruiser lately. "Gladenuff's our man, whatever his name really is. It sure ain't Benko Gladenuff. He's got a string of aliases as long as your income tax form."

The Chief cackled at his joke, staying on my case, letting me know he'd snooped into my tax filings and seen the novellas I submitted every April.

"The ID report on your boy finally came in. I can't believe how slow those guys in Washington are. They're supposed to have this immigrant tracking business under control by now. But they got a good excuse on this one: no immigrant. Ha!"

What did he mean? Gladonov wasn't from Russia?

The Chief rambled on. "Clement's just a dinky little town with no influence. I'm gonna let all the chiefs around the state know about the FBI's farting around while a murderer gets away. Don't know what good it will do, though."

Letting him vent, I rolled down my window and sniffed the moist, sparkling air. Whatever strange news he had couldn't faze me now. I don't know if I was still numb from all the stress or if I accepted deep-down that everything was all right now, but I'd become indifferent to the whole investigation. Whatever Buhrman knew, I couldn't do anything.

"No wonder Immigration couldn't find him. The file traces him back to New Jersey," Buhrman burst out, as excited as when he began the investigation. "It says he's Polish, born in Newark. His birth name is Robert Drinski. How do you like that?"

"Amazing." I sat up, clapped him on the shoulder, pretending enthusiasm. "Good job, Aaron. I wish I had you to check on all my employees with accents."

"Yeah," he said, so wrapped up in his story he missed my sarcasm. Just as well. I didn't need to maintain my adversarial attitude toward him any more. He was dismantling the entire case he'd built against me. "Jerk spent a couple of years in lockup in Newark when he was a kid. He must have learned a few tricks there. Once he got out, he developed a nice career as a thief and credit card con under the names like Peter Gleeno, Josev Frunoosky, William Vallerie, who knows who godforsaken else? Spent more time behind bars. He sure sounded Russian. Where'd he get the accent?"

"Who knows?" I said. "Who cares now?"

"Faked it really good."

"He spoke English like an ape," I said.

"Sounded Russian enough to me. Don't know too many foreigners, though. Puerto Ricans, Frenchies from Quebec, some of them Vietnamese. My wife gets her nails done by a little Vietnamese gal."

Buhrman slowed down and stopped for some pedestrians. He waved and smiled at them. They waved back and he said, "I wish he was a Russky, be easier to take. Gotta admit, he's one tricky asshole. Didn't know Polacks were so clever."

"Like I said a while back, he fooled us all. Don't feel too bad about it, Aaron."

"Feel bad? I don't feel bad. He's a social pathawlic."

I laughed at him. "Whatever he was, he was good at it."

"Fell out of sight in '97. Showed up in New York again. Detained at Kennedy Airport in 2000. When did he start working for you? Did you ever call any people he worked for? Try to find out who he really was?

"I told you the company in England gave him a stellar reference." "Probably a phony company," Buhrman grunted.

"How would I know that, Aaron?" I started to heat up. It felt good. I started to feel like my old self, wide awake and ready for anything. "Now what are you accusing me of?"

"Nothing, Charlie. Calm down. We just got conned. The Mac-Daniel woman got the worst of it." He'd driven us to the outskirts of town and pulled into the abandoned drive-in movie theater lot. He began circling the weedy field and slowly curving around and between bent and rusted poles that held the car speakers in the drive-in's hay-day.

We've all got our own ways or working off tension and if the Chief wanted to pretend he was a test driver weaving through an obstacle course, let him cruise the Clement archeology of the last century.

"What pisses me off is that I should have known. Nine times out of ten, it's the boyfriend. Soon as we knew he was screwin' her, we should have closed in. He just knocked her on the head and tossed her in the tank to make it fool us. Trouble was, she didn't have any signs of recent sexual penetration."

"It could have been an accident. We don't know if he did it. You're too emotionally involved. Stay objective."

He'd used every subtle form of intimidation and threat to throw me off base during his investigation and I intended to make sure the town council knew how he'd treated me.

"Bullshit. You have to be emotionally involved in a murder in your town. You have to care if you're going to get anywhere. If you don't, nobody will. Except maybe the victim's kids. Think about it, Greer."

He spun out of the drive-in parking lot, spraying gravel behind us like a hyped-up adolescent rebel.

I waited to speak until we cruised smoothly down the highway. "All I'm saying is, do you have enough proof?"

"We got more than enough circumstantial. Here's what happened: He bumped her off. Brought her into the factory to set up the accident. The Chinaman saw him. He threatened the Chink or paid him off to get out. All those foreigners connive together. I had him scheduled to come in for a second interview. If hypnosis didn't work out—I never figured it would. It was some fancy bureaucrat in the D.A.s office came up with that cockamamie idea."

"I wish you'd done it. I've never been in a trance before," I said. "I hear it can make you feel real good."

"Yeah. If you mean how good you feel if you stop smoking. Anyway, I planned to polygram the weasel. I told him I wasn't gonna wait till the hyp-nutter waved his watch. So when the heat started coming down, Gladpop split. We almost had him."

"Sounds feasible," I said.

"District Attorney likes it, too. It's true. That's what counts." "But it's just your opinion, Aaron."

"Charlie, when are you gonna get it? I'm a professional police officer," he said. "My opinion is the second most important thing in an investigation. The facts is first. Smell the coffee, Mr. Tofu Head. If you don't have a strong opinion about things in this world, the way it's changin' so fast, you're just a sheet flappin' the breeze."

"All right, Aaron." I didn't feel like arguing, but I let slip some words I almost regretted. "If you knew the truth, you'd be surprised."

"What d'ya mean?" snapped Buhrman, ever suspicious. "What're you saying, Charlie? Do you know something you ought to tell me?" He stared at me gimlet-eyed, as if he still held the power of threat over me. "I haven't closed the case yet. No statute of limitations on murder, y'know. Don't hold back any information. We're still all in this together. D. A.'s thinking about posting a national wanted bulletin on Gladenuff. If you have something, say it."

Our eyes locked. I shrugged. "I mean, everybody's a mystery, when it comes to who they really are. You never know what makes people do the things they do. Anyway ..." I stared out the windshield wondering how to neutralize the Chief's willingness to ride the case into the ground, with me under him. I saw why the District Attorney had stuck with him, even when he had only his hunches. So I said, "I don't know anything you don't."

He slowed the car and squinted at me, figuring some way to regain his authority over me. Then he shrugged and gave me a flat smile as if I'd never see the truth, even if I was knee-deep in it, smelling it stinking up the room around me. "We have one witness," he said, "only one, but she might be helpful someday."

"What? Witness to what?" Did someone see me that morning? "A neighbor. Mrs. Brakefield, lady who lives across the street.

She must be ninety-five. Never sleeps." He watched my reaction. "Did she see him leave or something?"

He's leading up to this. You were careless when you dragged Benko out of the house.

"Naw. Too bad. Nobody saw him leave. Can't figure out how he got away. No cab, no bus out of town, no plane flights under his name. That's no surprise. Left his car to fake everybody out. Guy musta had friends from out of town, picked him up and spirited him away. Probably a woman."

"What did the neighbor see?" This worried me.

"Women. Lots of women coming and going at all times, day and night. Two in particular. One of 'em big and fat. It was winter so I thought maybe she was wearing a parka or something. Other one she saw quite a bit last summer, she said. Little, long black braid, maybe brown. Old Mrs. said she was a runner-type, shorts, shiny headband."

That one could have been Nora. She liked to run the streets of town early in the morning or just after dusk. When she ran, she braided her hair and wore a reflective headband.

"Any idea who these women were?"

"Could be anybody. Maybe there was only one, the deceased. She had the long brown hair and the old lady got mixed up. She's not really a good witness. I talked to all the other neighbors, but nobody saw anything unusual. 'Course, he could have taken off with one of those women. Pity her."

"So it's over? You're done."

"Not quite. Too bad I don't have his DNA. Too late now to make a match to the fetus. That would cinch it, I think. Disrict attorney says he doesn't have the budget to scrape around his apartment and send it out. Until I have his confession, I can't say it's over. Like most of these cases."

"So I hear." The Chief belonged on the criminal investigation unit of some city where he could dog a dozen cases at the same time, pressing on until he earned the satisfaction of filing at least one of them in his "Closed" drawer. I wouldn't feel totally easy until he left Clement and forgot about the case of the 'murder' in the tofu factory.

As he pulled to the curb outside my office, he said, "About the other DNA? There's one thing you might as well know. Just keep it to yourself."

I waited.

"You heard we had some trouble with the lab?"

"They got the samples mixed up?"

"Right. Those Puerto Ricans got themselves so discomboobulated with their paperwork they forgot to do the real testing. I'da known it was a dead end if they'd done their job right in the first place. D. A. understands. He promised to handle it. But he's not gonna spend any more budget on Gladnoof."

"What are you talking about, Aaron?"

"That flesh we found under the MacDaniel woman's fingernails?"

"Yeah?"

"It doesn't tell us much."

I caught my breath. "It wasn't Gladonov's skin?"

"Naw." He drove in silence, glancing at me several times before he went on. "It was hamburger."

"Hamburger!" I coughed, covering my shock.

"Yeah. It must have gotten stuck under there when she made the patties for her birthday party."

"Jesus. Aaron, do you know what that means?" I clenched my stomach muscles to prevent a bitter laugh and to stop myself from snapping, "You built the whole investigation around some hamburger?" I couldn't hold my laughter in and I burst into a belly laugh, throwing my body in wild shakes.

Embarrassed and solemn, he said, "I'm charging you officially to keep this quiet. You must know what it's like to be surrounded by idiots, being in business, so many employees and all."

I inhaled a deep breath to cover my glee, and followed it with another and another. I turned my face to the window so I could roll my eyes and drop my mouth and let my face contort while I held the laugh down in my diaphragm.

He went on. "Once we find Gladpop, or Drinkski, or Popsicle Pete, whatever, we'll need him to think we've got DNA evidence."

"I don't know if you can bluff those guys, Aaron," I said, snorting, coughing. "They're sharper than your average Clementine."

"That's true. We're not innocents up here, but we aren't citified. We plan to keep it that way, however we can. We don't blame ourselves for getting stung by a pro. Next time, I'm gonna stick with tradition—work the boyfriend first and foremost."

"Good idea, Aaron," I said, chuckling as we pulled to a stop in front of the factory. Little did he know, he'd been working the boyfriend all along.

"Did you ever figure out the motive?"

"Ah, Greer. You're dense. The cupcake in the oven. He knocked her up and she wouldn't get rid of it. She had morals, that one."

"Plausible," I said.

"Yeah. Kinda weak for murder, I know. What else do we have? The guy was evil. DA says pathohawlics don't need much of an excuse."

Buhrman sat up straighter, bracing his shoulders back, staring through the windshield. We rode in silence for a few minutes.

"By the way, I heard that sales lady of yours left the company. Nice woman."

Did he think it an odd coincidence that Genevieve had moved out of town a few weeks after Benko left? The truth was her best cover. "It wasn't easy trying to build sales in the middle of your murder investigation. Still, she did one hell of a job. Time came for her to move on anyway. She got a great job out West."

"Go West young lady. I liked her."

I opened the car door. "Thanks for the ride, Aaron. I'll miss our afternoon excursions in the cruiser. Think sometime you could take my kids for a jaunt around town with the lights flashing? I told them about the big gun and the radio."

"We'll see. I gotta think what the taxpayers would say if I was tooling around with rich kids in the squad car."

I grimaced but shook Buhrman's hand and gave him the thumbs up sign with my other hand. As I climbed out of the car, he flicked on his blue lights and gunned the motor.

"One good thing came out of this," Buhrman said. "I'm a lot smarter now. It ever happens again? I'm on it day one."

"Glad to hear that, Aaron. Makes me feel a lot safer." I grinned at him and slapped the top of the cruiser as he squealed away with the lights flashing, siren starting up.

As the Chief dopplered away toward town, I strolled around the factory, noting a few repairs we'd do once spring bloomed. Replaying the Chief's revelations, I laughed to myself, giddy as a head case. Shivers ran up and down my back and I ran to the building, scrambling up the four-story ladder to the top of our refrigerated warehouse where I could luxuriate in full March sunlight.

On the roof, higher than the old oaks and pines that bordered our lot, I clambered on all fours up the shingles, scanning the empty fields beyond American Tofu as I climbed. At the peak, I perched and raised my arms and stretched them out wide. For that moment, if a strong wind blew my way, I could fly.

Epilogue

Charlie

DOWN AT THE RIVER

bad luck, an accident
it wasn't my fault it
was all my fault

I didn't kill Becky. We had an accident, that's all. I couldn't help it.

If anyone else knew what happened, I can understand how they might think I was responsible, and in some way, I was, but not guilty of any wrongdoing. You could blame it on lust or tequila, or on the night, for that matter. Hell, you could say the moss on the rocks was lying there all slippery, waiting for us. You could take it all the way back to the beginning of our lives and say dying's what we're born for.

But the truth is, when it comes down to blaming, you can only blame it on bad luck.

I was just beginning to love her, this natural, light-hearted woman who surely loved me already.

Since we fell for each other, we'd kept our affair secret, totally undercover, because I was a married man. We—that is, I, had too much to lose by announcing I'd fallen in love with my employee and was leaving my family for her.

After a couple of months of seeing each other, she became my favorite person, the one I could tell everything to, and she was the best lover I'd ever had. Not that I'd had many, but she made me open up and praise whatever God there is for turning me all inside out and washing me in light and then putting me back together as a better happier person.

I picked her up at nine thirty, after her birthday party with friends. She'd told them to go home early because she had to be at the plant by two and she needed a few hours of rest. Little did they know she'd saved her real celebration for me.

I'd called our sitter but she couldn't come over so I had to leave the kids sleeping. It wouldn't be the first time their mother and dad were gone at night, so they wouldn't worry if they woke up and found themselves alone for a few minutes.

Becky jumped into my old Cherokee as excited and happy as I'd ever seen her. We drove out of town and down a pitted gravel road that followed the river, bumping along under a thick forest canopy drizzled with so much moonlight I crept along with my lights out. Warm breeze and gurgling sounds from the shallow river seeped into the car as we approached our favorite parking spot.

Before we climbed out of the car, Becky put her hand on my arm and asked me, "Don't you feel like a fish tonight?"

Joking, I said, "Not really. More like a stallion." When I reached to touch her cheek, she caught my hand in her chapped fingers and held it in mid-air.

"No, seriously. I mean, right now, see those shadows? How they wiggle between the moonbeams? Like we're sitting in a fish net made of light and dark."

Her imagination astounded me. I'd always wanted to be a poet, and I wrote haiku all the time, but Becky saw magic in the world that every grown-up had forgotten long ago.

She uncapped her thermos of frozen margaritas and we sat drinking and toasting each other. Before long, we started giggling and laughing like idiots, as we always did. I never had more fun with anybody in my life.

We hopped down the root-stairs on the riverbank and stood in the shade of an enormous oak. I told Becky I wanted to cross the river so I could give her my present in style.

"I have a wonderful present for you, too," she whispered, kissing my ear.

"Hobbit's birthday present?"

"How did you guess? Just like a hobbit, on my birthday I'm giving you a present."

A jumble of rocks and boulders colored pewter by the moon lay exposed above the August brook. After hanging out at the river for so many years, I was used to stepping from boulder to boulder to cross the shallow riverbed, so I whispered the most disastrous words I'd ever said.

"Let me carry you over."

"Like a groom?" she said. "Or like a stallion?"

We laughed until we bent over, bouncing off each other. At the riverbank, Becky leapt up and swung her legs around my waist. Holding my neck in both hands, she threw her head back and howled. She was small but she felt heavy and a pain nagged at my lower back so I flipped her around to hold her lying across both of my arms, like the groom.

The first rock was dry and flat. The nearly full moon painted such a clear path across the riverbed, I could have danced on the rocks with my eyes closed and never missed a step.

Hugging her tight, I stretched across the wide gap between flat boulders near the middle of the river. As my foot touched down, my heel skidded out and shot across the rock. My leg slid off the boulder and slipped down into shin-deep water, my legs splitting apart and my arms flying up. I tried to angle myself under Becky so she would land on top of me but she pitched out of my arms and dived head-first into the stream shadows. I fell on my back, landing on a flat rock and snagging my ankle in a cleft between two others.

I sat there, my ankle and back throbbing, letting the tequila fog clear. "Becky. Becky. You okay? I hurt my ankle." She didn't answer. As I observed her sprawled on the exposed riverbed, water filled my shoes and soaked my shorts. A hot ache climbed my calf from my ankle, stabbing deep inside my kneecap like a thorn.

"Must have been moss on the rock. I'm sorry," I said, calm as the night was warm. "Hang on, I'm coming."

She lay glowing in milky moonlight with her head and hand thrown back into the darkness on the other side of the slippery granite. "God. Becky. Becky. Are you all right?"

She was unconscious. I crawled across the rocks as quickly as I could and picked her up, lifting her high, holding her back to my chest and slipping and sliding my way five or six painful steps to shore where I lay her out on the stony beach. Raising her head to check for blood or any crushed bone, all I found in the dim light was a bump about the size of a thumb tip beside her left eyebrow.

She lay too still, so after tapping her cheek and calling her name, I pressed my ear to her chest. When I heard her heart beating, I sat back on my haunches, relieved, but still worrying. Even if her head was uninjured, what about her back?

The boozy haze had settled in again so I slapped my head to clear it while my mind raced senselessly. I knew what I had to do, but my arms and legs could barely move. I had to get her to the hospital and damn the consequences. Just let her be all right. I'd figure out a believable story later. Just let her be all right.

The brook struggled among the rocks, gurgling and choking its way downstream. Every few seconds, I glanced over at Becky. I could barely see her chest rise and fall.

I caressed her cheek again. Kissing her eyelids, I slid my fingers into her damp hair and lifted her head gently. Kissed her on the lips again. Did she kiss me back? I thought she did. I finally lay her head back on the ground—it flopped to the side.

At that, my lungs quivered in my chest and began to tighten up as panic stole my breath. After hacking as hard as I could and pounding on my chest with my palm, my throat finally loosened.

When my breath came a little easier, I tried to find her pulse in her wrist. Nothing there, so I touched her neck, seeking her carotids on both sides. Her skin felt clammy and spongy so I yanked my T-shirt off and patted her neck and face until it dried. Then I listened to her heart again—nothing.

A relentless homophony of crickets jangled the cool river air, distracting me for a second with an illusion of tranquility. Then, a bullfrog croaked from the weeds a few feet away. I jumped up and stumbled around, peering into the frightful night, expecting someone to step out of a shadow.

I knelt back down, and forcing my ear deep into her chest between her breasts, I listened for a long time. Nothing.

Opening my mouth and placing it around her nose, I wanted to feel her breath, to taste it. Under my hand, her chest didn't move and she didn't make the slightest sound.

"Jesus. O my God. O shit." I opened my mouth and screamed but caught myself and shut up, then listened for her heartbeat once more, for a long minute.

Nothing.

I lay my head on her stomach, my legs spread out on the stony shore.

I tried my version of CPR, breathing into her nose and mouth then pressing down on her chest. The slow rhythm calmed me down a bit, but she wouldn't respond. Finally I pushed myself away and stood up, tiny stones and pebbles stuck to my sweaty thighs. I brushed them off, slapping at them and picking them out of my kneecaps one by one, listening, waiting for something. Becky to wake up? Time to stop? The river to reverse itself and flow upstream? How could this happen to me? What did she do to deserve this? What did I do?

I carried Becky to my car and lay her in the back seat, the last place we'd made love. In death she had shrunk somehow. Her body fit between the doors, making it easy for me to wedge her against the crease between the bench and the seat back.

I started the car and turned around on the moonlight-mottled road and, bouncing on potholes, we headed toward the emergency room that wouldn't do any good. Every few minutes, I twisted around to check on her.

Every time I glanced back, she lay there, eyes closed, one arm hidden under her, one arm splayed toward me, her legs bent and leaning against the seat. I reached and felt her pulpy hand as if I could assure her everything was going to be fine.

I loved her more on that drive than I had ever loved her and felt so pissed off at love that it couldn't bring her back. Pure, spontaneous love for a woman, a woman I wasn't married to, a woman I shouldn't have fallen for, but a woman I couldn't resist because she didn't care who I was or what I did or when I came home, the kind of love I had always wanted and didn't know how badly.

Now that love would wreck Nora's and Chuckie's and Marissa's lives, too. Would my business go down? Would I lose everything? What about Becky's kids? Who'd take care of them now? They were my kids' age and their father had left them years ago.

I drove, still dizzy from the tequila, thoughts hurtling through my brain. My natural skepticism and caution spiraled into a full-blown paranoia, thinking through the possible questions the police might come up with.

The police? My God, the police would get involved. It was an accident, no matter how it happened. People die in accidents all the time, car accidents, falls. What about the thousands of people doctors kill by giving them the wrong drugs? My problem was not the accidental part of her death—I wasn't supposed to be with her. If people found out, that's all she wrote for Charlie Greer. The cops would want to check my story out to the nth detail. They were paid to distrust me and not believe anything I said.

Boss and pretty worker, happens all the time. When they got that, I rise to the top of the suspect list.

I told myself over and over I should just tell the truth right now and accept the misery. The divorce. The humiliation. Lose everything and everybody. I'd never be able to hold my head up in public. My God, the headlines: "New York Entrepreneur of the Year Indicted for Murder." These small towns have infinite memories, especially about scandals like this one.

The Charlie Greer everyone knows and loves would not survive. If I told the truth, I might as well end it all myself.

Maybe Becky wasn't as virtuous and loving as I thought. Maybe she wanted my money. Maybe she thought of herself as the next Mrs. Charlie Greer, queen to his kingdom of tofu. I heard the last thing she said to me again: "Like a groom?" If everything went according to her plan, I'd be supporting her two kids and mine and paying alimony and giving half my hard-earned income and the few assets I have to Nora.

I crept along below the speed limit. My mind slipped off into anxious reveries and then I'd come to, my teeth clicking, goose bumps skittering on my arms and shoulders, my car crawling along at ten miles an hour down streets I'd driven a hundred times before. But that night, I'd never been there before.

At least I didn't drive off the road and crash into a tree. Maybe that's how I should handle this, wreck the car, bloody my head and let Becky get thrown out onto the pavement where she smashes her head and dies?

The idea tempted me. Becoming lucid for a moment, I realized that if I tried that, first, I could get hurt and the situation would then be totally out of my control with gossips and cops having their way. Second, if I didn't get hurt, with Becky dead, people might guess it was a staged accident.

The closer we came to the hospital, the woman in the back seat became less Becky and more a body, a dense thing, the worst possible luck a man could have, short of losing his children. That body didn't belong on my earth. The inert flesh and bones back there reviled me no matter how much I'd loved the woman.

We approached the blinking yellow light at the hospital corner and I slowed down further.

I shivered and turned the opposite way and accelerated away from the hospital. No matter what happened now, old Charlie had to handle it on his own.

***

I pulled into my driveway and parked beside the garage on Chuckie's basketball court. I backed in, angling close to the tall lilac bushes.

Before climbing out of the car, I squeezed Becky's hands and legs. I guessed I had a few hours before rigor mortis set in. Rolling the body into the leg space between the seats, I covered it with the picnic blanket.

Limping inside, I swallowed four ibuprofen and showered in scalding water for as long as I could stand it. I still had half an hour before my wife showed up. I paced around my bedroom in the gloom.

I noticed the leather Bible Nora kept in her bedstead. I opened it to Samuel saying "God do so to me, and more also ... " I threw the book down. I didn't need an eye-for-an-eye judgment in my own bedroom. The outside world would supply more than enough.

Spotting my favorite haiku collection, I picked it up from my bedside table. I thumbed it open to tragic old haiku man Issa and read "In the heart of this everyday world we stroll along the roof of hell gawking at flowers."

Unable to bear literary truth, I dropped the book and went into the bathroom again. I turned on the bright make-up lights over the mirror and palmed a circle clear of moisture left over from my shower. I wanted to see my face, to assure myself that whatever happened, I was the same Charlie Greer, a man who met life's uncertainties head-on—Charlie never flinched.

My face resembled the same guy of a few hours ago whose biggest problems in life were making money and finding love, but I barely recognized him. His baggy eyes bugged out and glittered like a scared, pissed-off cat after some kid threw him in a tank of cold water.

I checked the kids in their rooms, imagining what it would be like if they grew up with their dad in jail for killing somebody. Whether he meant to kill or not, it wouldn't make any difference to them. "Killer's kids." They'd have to move far away and they'd never be able to visit me.

I knelt beside Chuckie's bed gazing into the face of innocence; nothing bothered him in his dream world. On the bedside table, the illuminated clock face shone through his transparent bowl of sea monkeys, his latest favorite toy. He'd raised three batches in the last month, and none had survived to jump around his room, as he insisted they would, if only he found the right food. The latest batch lay inert, clumped together at the bottom of the bowl.

I kissed Chuckie on his hot cheek and pulled his blanket down so he wouldn't overheat and have nightmares.

Rissi heard me come through her door.

"Daddy?"

Her voice opened the floodgates on the pond of sorrows I'd stored up for my whole life. As a rivulet of tears pressed up and leaked out of my eyes, I coughed, "Hi sweetie."

"Hi Daddy."

She turned over and hugged her 'Georgie,' the sock monkey her grandma made, her bedtime companion since she left Nora's and my bed four years ago. A beam of moonlight shined through the gap between the window shade and the sash and fell across her baby face, a blessing from the all-loving night.

My baby girl, my princess, safe and peaceful and gorgeous and all the world waiting to give you love and happiness. Oh, baby, I have totally wrecked your life. God help me.

I kissed her on the chin, then on the lips. A single tear dripped off my eyelash and fell onto her face. It rolled down her cheek and she brushed at it, like at a mosquito.

I stood there, trembling, and the thought of Becky's little girl came to me, motherless, red-haired like her mom, sleeping at some aunt's or friend's house with her doll tucked under her chin never again having a mother to watch over her and kiss her good night. I sagged against the wall wanting to let myself slide to the floor and fall asleep, forgetting all the misery I was causing.

Instead, I went back into the bathroom and stuck my head in the sink. I ran icy water over my skull and neck, chilling back tears and shrinking the puffiness around my eyes, in case Nora noticed. Then I climbed into bed and turned onto my stomach with the sheet pulled up to my ears, my mind now half-paralyzed from sorrow.

At exactly eleven thirty, Nora's car turned into the driveway. She came into the house and upstairs to the bedroom where I was faking sleep with a pillow over my head. She climbed in beside me. Thank God it takes her two minutes to drop into an eight-hour coma.

The customary sound of her breathing started to lull me into an alpha state and I almost faded out. Forcing myself to stay awake, tossing and turning with eyes open, I imagined Becky lying in my car. I could almost hear Becky calling my name.

'Charlie? Come get me. It's cold out here. I need your arms around me. It's my birthday, remember?'

I bolted up in bed. What kind of present was she going to give me? Did she leave something in the car? I had to make sure I cleaned out mud or leaves or her smell on the blanket—I'd have to throw it away. Did she have a purse when I picked her up? Did she tell anybody she was going out with me tonight? One of her girlfriends? Shit. I hoped to hell I didn't leave the margarita thermos at the river.

If someone's in the know, where you gonna go?

It was true, I had no place to go. If I disappeared, I'd be admitting guilt and be running for the rest of my life. Maybe I should just take her home and dump her in her back yard. Let somebody find her and the cops will figure that somebody at her party killed her.

Too many lights in her neighborhood. A lot of people in Clement would recognize my license plate "Tofu 4 U." No way I can drive up to Becky's front door in the middle of the night now and carry her body over my shoulder into her house.

Maybe I'll take Becky to the river and lay her on the rocks. Come back and get her car and abandon it there. Make it seem like she went out there by herself after her party and she slipped and did herself in.

I almost got out of bed until I thought, Stupid, how're you gonna get out to the river, do whatever, and walk back to town to get Becky's car? Too complicated. Somebody will see you wandering around the streets.

Bad luck Charlie Greer. All you can do is cry a tear.

Had to get myself under control and make a plan but my mind was paralyzed.

She ain't comin' back from the afterlife. You better figure out how to make the deal of your life.

Panicked whispers flooded my mind. I listened hard but all I could make out was a rush like wind in the trees. The sound soothed me. For a moment, I calmed down and I drifted toward sleep again, giving in to everything that had happened. I stretched my legs and tensed all my muscles, then let them go soft, allowing my body to separate from my head so I could think clearly.

At that moment, it came to me: I saw exactly what I had to do. It was what Becky would want me to do. Because she loved me, she wouldn't want me or my family or hers hurt any more. My heartbeat quickened and my thoughts cleared as I understood that if I played my cards right, I could make everything turn out the best way it could, for all of us, except Becky, of course.

She'd had an accident. Yes. Simple. Only it was an industrial accident—factories are dangerous places, everyone knows that, even tofu factories. For the next ten minutes, every step of a risky, but doable plan unfolded as I watched and listened and tweaked details. I checked at the clock. Twelve seventeen. I'd have time. It would take less than an hour to pull off what I decided to do that night—for Becky, for our kids, for all of us.

***

I climbed out of bed, as I did in the middle of many nights. If Nora noticed me gone from the room, she'd think I was downstairs, maybe in the yard.

Checking the back seat, I felt relieved, almost happy, to find Becky's body still there. Wincing at my morbid reaction, I got in and saw the margarita thermos on the floor of the passenger side, but nothing else. No purse. Things were looking up.

In ten minutes, we arrived at my tofu factory where she was due for work at two. The sour smell of her clothes overwhelmed the naturally rich perfume of the leather upholstery.

I circled the parking lot to make sure all the night shift cars had left. Every night, for the hour between one and two, the building was completely empty.

I pulled up close to the factory side door and punched in the security code. I tugged Becky out of the car and hoisted her over my shoulder and started across the production room, a walk I'd taken almost every working day for the last seven years. The pain in my ankle had subsided and the bang on my tail barely throbbed.

Inside the hollow factory, the hideous moonlight shined down through the windows near the ceiling and glinted off a forest of stainless steel tanks and pipes, disorienting me again.

I shuffled through the murky plant, passing from shadows into slanting silvery beams and back into the gloom. I slipped once or twice on the floor, nearly tripping on the puddles. My steps scudded across the tile, sounding distant from my body, as if the echoes of someone else's feet followed me.

I entered the women's dressing room and flipped on the light and lay Becky gently on the floor. While stripping off her shorts and blouse, I avoided her face. She wore a lacy black bra and black silk bikini panties.

I sensed her spirit lingering near us the way they say they do when someone dies violently and unexpectedly. I don't believe in ghosts, I don't believe in any afterlife, but if, just in case, her life force hadn't evaporated and it could sense my intentions, I felt she'd do everything she could to help me, to protect me, as long as I still loved her and handled everything the best I could.

I noticed my watch and saw that I didn't have much time before the crew arrived. I stood up and nearly fell over. Not the booze this time. I waited with my eyes closed and my stomach clenched, but nothing came up.

In a minute, I opened Becky's locker and slipped her white production uniform off the hanger and pushed and tugged it up over her legs and arms. My fingers trembled so fiercely I could barely button the blouse. I arranged her cold, sodden party clothes on the hanger and hung them in her locker. They reeked of smoke from her barbecue.

I lifted her up and held her in a tender hug. I kissed her rubbery cheek and her cold nose and lay my lips against hers. Her icy mouth stung and I jerked away, gagging.

Buck up, Chuck.

I blew hard out my mouth, spluttering and spitting. I had to overcome my body's reaction to the dead body, my fear of what was coming. I had to get back to work.

I bent over to throw her body over my back and I eased my shoulder under her middle and tried to straighten up. She was wasn't too heavy but I was weak-kneed and my sore ankle buckled and my chin slammed into the floor. Groaning, I grunted and eased myself up.

I plodded out of the dressing room into production area trying to hold her away from my body but with every shuffling step I took, she flopped against me.

We approached the huge vats of soaking soybeans. Softening for processing, the beans smelled like yesterday's oatmeal.

I climbed up the steps to the open top of the five hundred gallon bean immersion tank. Four tons of hydrated soybeans lolled plump and ready for transformation into tofu. I opened the hinged lid and hefted Becky's body up over the lip of the tank and heaved, pushing her head, face-first, into the beans in the center of the tank.

As soon as I let the body go, it floated, bulging above the beans like a bubble of gas. Her hair, buoyed up by the two inches of water that covered the beans, spread into a dark red halo rippling around her skull.

I leaned over, bracing my knees against the wall of the vat and pressed her shoulders and head down into the beans.

One forty five.

As I rushed across the production room toward the glowing red exit sign, I glanced back at the bean soaking tank and its tragic contents. Silhouetted against the gleaming white wall, Becky's boot soles appeared above the vat staring at me like Kilroy eyes.

I laughed. A bark echoed back at me from the across the room. I stifled another laugh rising from my belly. I was losing it.

I let myself out, punched in the code, and drove home, my teeth chattering all the way.

In my yard, I sat in the kids' swing set until I calmed down. Listening to the crickets call incessantly for their mates, I gave in to prayer.

> *Becky, there's no way but please forgive me. You know we really fucked up. I didn't mean it. You were too wiggly. Your kids, O, my god, please forgive me. Nora, you can never know about this. Please forgive me. Jesus, Buddha, Great Spirit if you're there, please let me survive. Let us. Help me find a way to make this right.*

> *Anything, I'll do anything. Just let it go away. Don't let my kids ever know about this. Do with me what you have to. Let me make it up to you some other way. I'll do everything I can for her kids. Please.*

Finally, I realized I'd better go inside and pretend to have a normal night sleeping in bed with my wife. Hand over hand on the banisters, I hauled myself up the stairs and into the bedroom and stripped and threw my clothes into the hamper. I'd have to wash them myself before Nora saw them and got curious about the mud.

I glanced up the street out the bedroom window, convinced that someone would drive up the road looking for me. The pale light obscured the borders between trees and hedges and their shadows. I sank onto the mattress and worked my legs under the sheet and lay limp beside Nora feeling like I'd run five marathons. My thigh muscles fluttered.

I willed myself to fall asleep but Becky's sad face lying on the riverbank glowed inside my closed eyelids. My sweet little Rissi's moonlit sleeping face alternated in my mind's eye with Becky's beautiful dead face. Tears flowed down my temples into my ears. Shivers ran through my scalp.

I held Rissi's image in my mind, focusing on her smile, because I was afraid to think about what would happen tomorrow and she was the most wonderful thing about my life, my purest inspiration for anything good about me.

Eventually, exhaustion saturated every nerve and I went numb. I lost sight of Rissi as a cloud passed over and swept her image into shadow.

The leaves in the maple outside stirred and a damp breeze blew through the open window. I pulled the sheet up to my chin and glanced at the clock: 2.04. I had a little time until somebody called from the plant with the bad news. I rolled over on my stomach and tried to sleep.

THE EMERALD TINCTURE

down at the river
where all my tofu starts
my secret wrongs, my sacrificial rites

I took a few days off after the Chief suspended the case. One cloudy afternoon, I found myself parked at Becky's and my favorite spot along the river. Plows had piled the snow four feet high on each side of the road and the wind scattered random flakes across my windshield.

I shut the car off and slogged over the snow banks and slid down the icy root staircase to the stream. Two or three courses of unfrozen water weaved among the boulders and flowed downstream to the reservoir that fed the tofu factory. All American Tofu was made with pure water from this little river.

That morning, I'd retrieved the maroon velvet jewelry case from my safe deposit box. Inside, I kept the birthday emerald earrings I never had a chance to give to Becky.

I stepped onto the ice, crossing the rocks, retracing my blundering steps when I'd held her warm living body in my arms. In a fit of self-punishment, I slipped both feet into the stream. Standing there, I cupped the earrings in my fist for a long time, then I opened my palm and stared at the sparkling green stones, the only color in the day.

A cold ache rose from my soaked feet up into my shins. My knees shook. I squatted down on the same flat rock I'd slipped on last summer and gazed for a long moment at the black water.

Just a matter of time, you'd end up at the scene of the crime.

A gust of frigid wind nearly knocked me backwards off my heels. I clasped my hands together over the jewels and rolled them back and forth. The earrings bit at my chilled skin, but the friction heated and softened my palms.

A crow flew by, wondering if the crazy human would leave any tasty morsels. He squawked and winged off.

I checked the earrings once more and joining my palms, held them in front of my chest and shook them together, hard. Like tiny dice, they clicked, but so softly I barely heard them above the splashing water.

I opened my hands for a last view of the fatal jewels. Then, I stretched my arms out and tipped my palms inward. The earrings slid into the indifferent river. They seemed to float for an instant. My fingers darted out, but the jewels sank into oblivion.

Now, all the tofu we make has water infused with the Becky MacDaniel emerald memorial. Everyone who eats American Tofu carries the mystical essence of Becky in their cells. It's a bizarre way to give somebody immortality—only in my mind.

No way the tincture's enough. Soy to the World? No. Nothing could ever be enough.

But what else is a tofu man to do?

Letter from San Francisco

Dear Charlie and Nora,

It took me a while to want to get in touch with you guys, but you understand. I think about you and AT and everything a lot and my therapist told me I'd probably be able to make peace with American Tofu in two years or so.

So now it's been more than two years, and I'm not ready to make full peace but I do want you both to know I still love you and most of all, I forgive all of us — well, there's one person I'll never forgive no matter if it corrupts my soul.

I forgive you Charlie for being an impulsive crazy ambitious narcissist because you have guts and you go for what you want and you do care about everyone else, even if it's in your own odd way. Maybe you've learned by now that just because you want it, it's not necessarily the right thing.

I forgive you Nora for being so complacent and not grabbing Charlie by the ears a long time ago and insisting he be honest with you, and for you being so dishonest with him, as if you guys had such a stable marriage you could weather any problems, like stupid affairs. Not that I'm innocent in the world of affairs—

Speaking of marriage, here's some cool news: I'm engaged. Not the ring way, with big wedding plans. No. We're totally heart to heart, nothing held back. Nothing. (Except one thing)

He's a combination painter-sculptor and biomedical entrepreneur. He's 45, has 2 kids by his baby-making marriage, loves me and I love him. I could go on and on about the handsomest man on the planet, Roberto Daniel Murakami. But I won't. Neither of us believe in marriage, but we believe the two of us (often the five of us) can create and live a beautiful life together for the rest of it.

Best news: Liam is now sort of in ninth grade—I'm homeschooling him with ten other families. Liam has the run of the city, or better said, the skateboard of the city. He has two wonderful close friends and countless other kids he spends time with. If you haven't already, you could check out his website and Facebook to see the beautiful wild videos he makes with his friends. He has the photographer's gift of perspective and structure, but his imagination is far cleverer than mine. He's happy.

So am I. My home is great—on Linda Street, a quiet little street in a nice section of town. I work a lot from my home office. My boss owns the house but he's giving me equity for my rent. Not bad. Needless to say, my job is perfect. I'm about to publish a cookbook (finally) featuring fusion recipes with vegetables and fruits and sauces very few people know about yet. I spend about eight weeks a year traveling, meeting chefs and farmers and ordinary people on four continents so far. They share their recipes with me—sort of like cooks did for me with the tofu cookbook. I often supply the recipes and voila! It'll be called Genevieve's Kitchen – Palette of the World. Pun intended, Charlie.

Remember when I used to play with romanesco and samphire? Well, get ready America—Gen's genius has finally been freed. By the way, Charlie, I love what dragon fruit and tiger nuts do for tofu. (I know you're going to come up with some crazy tiger nut promotion Charlie but please don't ask me to create any more tofu recipes.)

Gianni is still my best friend, tho we haven't seen each other in person for a while. We still talk almost every week. He mentioned American Tofu seems to be taking over the universe. You're all over the country and shipping to Mexico?

Okay, you guys. How are Rissi and Chuckie? Show them Liam's work. They'll be inspired and will get it better than we do. They'll know how to get in touch with him if they want to.

Most important, are you being good and loving to each other?

I'm still not ready to see either of you—too much trauma trigger. I've only been sleeping all night for a few months, so ...

I just want you to know I love you both. Please write me especially with your kids' news and a little bit about how you are. I'll write back but let's not rush communications.

I'm sure you're still in recovery mode, Nora. I'd appreci-ate a short note about how you're doing.

It sounds like Charlie, you're still a mad achiever, must be your own brand of therapy. Not so sure if it goes very deep, but you're your own guy, one of the most unique characters I've ever met.

much love, your friend always

Genevieve

The End

Book Three

Down at the River

THE HOUR BETWEEN ONE AND TWO

The author

Thomas Timmins has published and performed his poetry and short fiction in person and in print across the U.S. and on the internet. He founded Fractals, a literary tabloid, cofounded and ran Poets & Players, a performance venue, developed and taught writing and coaching programs for inmates, published commercial writing, and founded and managed small businesses ranging from soyfoods to ice cream to telephone fundraising to biological pest control to a video game start-up to energy efficiency retrofits and a media company.

www.thomastimmins.com